The Light-Bearer and the Darkness

Ancestors' Shame

J.C. Moore

KENCEE
PUBLISHERS
CONYERS, GEORGIA

THE LIGHT-BEARER AND THE DARKNESS

ANCESTORS' SHAME

———

J.C. Moore

Library of Congress Control Number: 2026908623

KenCee Publishers Paperback ISBN:978-1-948502-05-4

KenCee Publishers eBook ISBN: 978-1-948502-08-5

Praise For J.C. MOORE

"WOW! *The Light-Bearer* is a gripping tale that harbors danger, death, fear, and hope. A must read!" —Tonya K. Grant, Author

"The story overtakes your mind and transports you intently to the *Mother* continent with vivid woven imagery." —Anita Jefferson, ED.M, Author of Climb Every Obstacle: Eliminate Your Limits!

"Get ready for a trip to our ancestral past replete with kings, princes, strained loyalties, and betrayals." —Stephana I. Colbert, Jewell Jordan Publishing

"When it ended, I wanted more!" —Alesia Crosby-Johnson, Founder & CEO of Kids Video Connection

"A poetic ode and wonderful read, filled with exquisite symbolism and a feast for the soul." —Patrick 'Preacher' Duncan, Scobie Entertainment

"The saying that the past isn't really past comes to life in this powerful page-turner that links the lives of an average American family with those of their African ancestors." —Sandra Davis, HBCU News

With gratitude to GOD — Great Omniscient Divinity.

*To Dr. and Mrs. Moore, my parents,
and Aaron Hamilton, my nephew.
To Najah, Cyril, Jr., Stephanie, Joseph,
Edward, Sr., and Clement, my siblings.
To Cousin Joan, Cousin Jean, Stephana, Tonya, TeMika, Scott, Alesia,
Kansas, Eloise, Tanisha, Nina, Maughtlyn, Paulette, Brenda, Patrick,
Anita, Dr. Jen, Sharon, Brenda, and Barbara.*

*To Louise, Gene, Teresa, Michael, Myguail, Shirley, Linda, Esther
(Rest in Peace) and the Friends of Stonecrest Library Book Club.
To AAGHS, Tia and BWC, Patricia and the Tubman Museum.*

*Special thanks to Sydellia N'Diaye, who assisted with my Wolof
(Senegalese) pronunciations and phonetics.*

*To Cheikh Anta, Ivan, Ishakamusa, Molefi, Kemet Nu, Ashra and
Merira and our ancestors who dwelt in the true Garden of Eden —
Alkebulan.*

Author's Note

"It is a historical truth. No man can know where he is going unless he knows exactly where he has been and exactly how he arrived at his present place." —Maya Angelou

We, the African diaspora, generally know how our ancestors arrived in the Americas and elsewhere. But relatively few of us have ever visited Africa, and even fewer have repatriated.

Yet, despite the centuries of separation, we remain tethered to our homeland. Neither slavery nor colonialism severed our ancestral umbilical cords. The continent is the mother we long to know.

It would be wonderful to pinpoint our lineage to specific families rather than general regions of Africa. *Ancestors' Shame*, the first in *The Light-Bearer and the Darkness* series, imagines such a feat.

This book pays homage to both the written and oral traditions of passing down history. It features people from ancient empires, such as the Baol and the Waalo. It also touches on historical events, such as Nasir Al-Din's Marabout Jihad, which was a holy war against the enslavement of Africans. However, the individuals and societies described are fictionalized composites.

Ancestors' Shame introduces the Daye family, who live in 21st-century America. Their lineage extends back to the powerful N'Diaye dynasty. This story unfolds in 17th-century West Africa, where the Great Lamane (king) of Lebu'ta, a fictional nation, strives to secure his timid grandson's succession to power whilst protecting his people and nation.

The Lamane and many African (Alkebulan) rulers faced hard choices: align with privateers from faraway lands, battle hostile neighboring kingdoms alone, or navigate shifting alliances with the Marabouts. The wrong choice could plunge Lebu'ta into the darkness rapidly covering the entire continent. But who to trust? Is there a light-bearer in Lebu'ta?

Join me in Ancestors' Shame, the first installment of *The Light-Bearer and The Darkness* series and stay with me to the last. It is a journey of a lifetime.

Ancestors & Descendants

Phonetic Pronunciations

"And whatsoever the man called each living
creature, that was its name."

—Genesis 2:19

People, Places and Things

21st CENTURY

CHARACTERS
Dame Daye - *Da-muh Day*
Abdoulaye "Abdo" Daye - *Ah-bah-do-lie Day*
Aminata "Ami" Daye - *Ah-min-not-tah Day*

THINGS
The Book - *Copper-encased pages of glyphs*
N'Diaye Dynasty - *N-jiye or N-g-yay Dye-nesti*

17th CENTURY

CHARACTERS
Karenga - *Kah-reng-gah*
Ahmed - *Ah-med*
Adama - *Ah-da-maa*
Kilifa Ibrahima - *Kih-lee-fa Ee-braye-ma*
Cheikh Anta - *Sh-ai-huh* Aen-tah
Awa - *Ah-wuh*
Mambéty Diop - *Mom-betty Dj-op*
Gueweel Griot Gorgui - *Gue -wuhl Gree-oh Gore-ghee*
Djibril - *Jih-bril*
Samba - *Sam-bah*
Malick - *Ma-leek*
Moustapha - *Moo-stah-fah*
Garmi - *Ga-arm-ee*
Bamba - *Bam-bah*
Sidy - *See-dee*
Zenaga - *Zen-ah-gah*
Signare Maguette - *Ceen-yar Ma-get*
Signare Alimatou - *Ceen-yar Al-lee-ma-too*
Oumou - *Oo-moo*
Aicha - *Ay-sha*

HISTORICAL AFRICANS
Burba N'Diadiane N'Diaye - *Bourr-ba Nja-djane Njiye (Wolof king)*
Nasir Al-Din (aka Nāir al-Dīn) - *Nah-sear Ah-hil-din (1644—1674)*

PEOPLE
Waalo - *Waah-lo*
Baol - *Bah-wool*
Serer - *Sei-rare*
Jolof - *Jo-loff*
Wolof - *Woh-loff*
Banju - *Ban-jewh*
Lebu - *Leh-boo*
Vumbi - *Vom-Bee (invented word: person, or people, from Europe)*
Métis - *Meh-teece (person of mixed-race)*
Signare - *Ceen-yar (wealthy, métis businesswomen)*
Marabout - *Mur-aye-bit or Ma-ra-boo (Pre-colonial West African Islamic leader)*

PLACES
Lebu'ta - *Le-boo-tah (fictional nation-state)*
Baobab Forest - *Bay-oh-bab Four-est (fictional forest)*
Alkebulan - *Alkebu-lan (Africa, mother of mankind)*
Île de Gorée aka Bir - *Ill-day-gor-ray aka beer (Island used for slave trading.)*

TITLES
Lamane - *La-mon (king)*
Maam bu góor - *Maahm-boo-gorr (granddad)*
Maam bu jigéen - *Maahm-boo-jee-ghen (grandma)*
Pape - *Pa-puh (dad)*
Yaye -*Ya-ee (mom)*
Le Capitaine - *Lee Kah pee-tan (the captain)*
Dom ou badjeen - *Dom-ooh-bah-jen (cousin from aunt)*
Dom ou nijaye - *Dom-ooh-knee-jaye (cousin from uncle)*
Gueweel (Wolof) aka Griot - *Historian, preserver of genealogies*

THINGS
Bukki - *Boo-key (hyena)*
Mabuyu - *Moo-bah-you (treat made from baobab)*
Marabout Jihad - *Mur-aye-bit or Ma-ra-boo Je-haad (Islamic holy war 1644-1674)*
Livres - *Lee-vrah (French currency 781-1794)*
Djembe -*Jem-beh (skin-covered wood, fashioned into a goblet-shaped drum)*
Glyph - *Glif (symbol; figure that conveys information)*
Cowrie - *Cow-ree (glossy, brightly colored shells; a.k.a. cowry)*
Poisoned darts - *Projectiles treated with poison for hunting and warfare*

THINGS (*continued*)
Baobab tree - *Bay-oh-bab (native to Africa; edible fruit, used to make paper, cloth, rope, also known as the Tree of Life)*
Flank - *Military maneuver; attack from one or more sides*
Fluyt - *Flute (Dutch sailing vessel designed to maximize cargo space)*
Rosetta Stone - *Glyphs in granite used to decipher ancient Kemetic medu neter aka Egyptian hieroglyphs (writings)*
Luminosity - *loo-min-os-ity (A system of passing down royal family histories)*
Talon Blade - *a fictional boomerang-type weapon with two curved blades*

Part One

Dynasty Discovered

"The drums of Africa still beat in my heart."

—Mary McLeod Bethune

Chapter 1

It Begins...

United States, North America — 21st Century

Sunlight gained entry through parted paisley curtains. Warm rays spread across the Daye's spacious kitchen. It reflected amber puddles on the lacquered table upon which a large metal-covered book sat. The encased sheaf of papers looked like a museum artifact. Thick, hammered copper cradled yellowed pages, wavy with age.

The door behind the table swung open. Dame Daye entered his family's kitchen from the garage. He dropped his key fob on the table and plopped into a chair.

"I am home," he yelled out. No one answered.

Hmm. What's this? He reached for the book.

Dame ran his hand over the dips and grooves of the reddish-orange metal. It felt pleasantly cool.

He picked it up and turned it to examine the strange, hinged binding. The uneven pages parted, and two sheets of notebook paper slid onto the kitchen table.

Dame put the book down and plucked up one of the two pages. He recognized his son Abdo's sloppy handwriting. He read the note.

Dad,
You're reading this letter, so I'm missing or dead. If Ami isn't with you, then she may be dead, too.

But you can still save the family. This book is the key. You'll see some pages are blank. They did not start that way. Little symbols had filled each page. Then something happened, and they disappeared.

Well, that's not quite right. They did not disappear. They're inside of me—a part of me. They just came off the pages, and I inhaled them.

Crazy, right? But it's true. I swear!

I know things I shouldn't know, couldn't know. The history of our family, our people, are clear, real memories—part of my own memories.

But I couldn't finish the book. That's why I stopped to write this note. I need you, Dad, to read the rest of the book. All of it.

The key is knowing and speaking their names aloud after reciting the oath to the ancestors. I will write as many names as I can, starting with our own.

Our last name, our true family name, isn't Daye but N'Diaye. That's right, like the ancient rulers of the Lebu'ta empire. I mean, we are descendants of an ancient African dynasty. How cool is that?

Mom always said you were her king. But she can't do it. She's not a N'Diaye. You're the only one who can do this.

Recite the oath to the ancestors, speak the names on the list, then read the rest of the book.

Trust me Dad, and read the book.

Abdo

Chapter 2

Recite The Oath

Dame stared hard at his son's signature. *What kind of game was Abdo playing?*

He crumpled the note and drew his arm back. "Abdoulaye, Aminata!" he bellowed and threw the paper, which landed near the trash can. Dame used the twins' full names. *Enough foolishness.*

There was no reply, no suppressed laughter or giggles — just his own breathing. Dame frowned. The silence plucked his nerve.

Dame pulled his cell phone from his pocket. He speed-dialed Abdo. The call went directly to voicemail. *That boy forgot to charge his phone again.*

He speed-dialed Ami. Voicemail.

He called his wife and received a call-reject text message: `In meeting. Call u later.`

Dame tossed the phone on the table. It spun until it bumped against the seven-inch spine of the book.

Dame looked away. His eyes landed on the crumpled page of Abdo's note he had thrown. The second page still lay on the table. He picked it up. His hand shook slightly as he struggled to concentrate on his son's scrawl.

This is the list, Dad. I've written it how it sounded when pressed into my mind. It's important to get it right. Something happens when you say their names aloud. You'll see what I mean.

Recite this oath to the ancestors first, then say their names.

Good ancestors. Our ancestors. You who are lamanes, builders, healers, warriors, gueweel griots, and keepers of mysteries. Reveal the secrets of the past. Impart to me the luminosity. Unite my mind with yours...

Prince Adama, son of Cheikh Anta N'Diaye
Princess Awa, daughter of Mambéty Diop
Lamane Kilifa, leader of Lebu'ta
Burba N'Diadiane, Pape of all

There's more, but there's no time now.

Abdo

Dame spoke the oath softly. The air vibrated when he said the first name on Abdo's list. Dame noticed the movement, yet continued to read aloud. He watched as his voice traveled on rays of sunlight and blanketed the book. Goosebumps pushed up every hair on his arms.

The book's copper cover glowed like smelting gold, then clanged open. Dame sprang from the chair. It toppled. He sidestepped the chair legs and moved away from the table. The blank pages turned quickly as if by a manic invisible hand. A quarter of the way through, the turning stopped.

Dame stood staring at the open book. *What the hell is going on? Are the kids really in some kind of trouble or is this one of Abdo's elaborate tricks?*

The silence weighed down Dame's mental acuity. *I need to do something. Look for them. Maybe call the police? I must do something!* He thought these things, yet remained rooted to the spot.

Dame's eyes locked on the book that beckoned him. Its uneven, wavy pages, like lips, seemed to smile seductively. All he wanted to do was read the book. He righted the chair, sat down, and pulled the open book towards himself.

The left page was blank. Dame peered at the small symbols on the opposite side. So many tiny glyphs. He turned the page and scanned row by row. First, right to left, and then in reverse. It was how he solved the *Find the Word* puzzles.

Dame recognized some of the symbols. A bird. A snake. A sickly sort of eye that seemed jaundiced on the old paper. But what did they mean?

This is impossible. How can I decipher these symbols without help? A Rosetta Stone-type reference or something? There's got to be hundreds of glyphs on just one page. And the damn book is huge!

Dame groaned. For a moment, just a moment, he did expect the images to come alive as Abdo had written. Just jump off the pages, enter his body, and solve the problem of his missing kids.

What am I doing? I've got to get a grip. He moved to shut the book.

The eye-shaped glyph blinked.

"What the..." Dame picked up the book and peered at the eye. It stared back — stoic, hypnotic.

His thoughts dimmed as the book's inner light brightened. The glyphs floated off the paper. Then, like orchestral instruments, all the symbols swirled in symphonic unison.

Mesmerized, Dame felt dizzy. Hundreds of glyphs entered his nostrils and stamped new memories on his mind. Dame's consciousness tore from his body, drifted upward, and hovered near the ceiling.

Dame briefly looked down at himself, holding the book, then he took flight.

Beneath him, subdivisions, skyscrapers, and freeways flattened. Time stretched and pulled Dame backward. Wavy ocean-blues melted into stucco forest-greens. He entered the land of his ancestors, where animals foraged, poisoned darts flew, and people hunted people.

Dame's consciousness glided over the tops of large African baobab trees. Somehow, he knew this place. Dame turned the page of the sacred book telepathically. He saw a blur of movement and heard faint buzzing sounds.

He wanted to cry out a warning, but the small word stuck in his disembodied throat. Dame mentally coughed and spat it out like phlegm. *Run!*

Part Two

Lebu'ta

"The black man in Africa had mastered the arts and sciences. He knew the course of the stars in the universe before the man up in Europe knew that the earth wasn't flat."

—Malcolm X

Chapter 3

...And Begins Again

Lebu'ta, West Africa (Alkebulan) — 17th Century

nap. The twig broke under fleeting pressure. No other sound was audible on the rarely used trail. Karenga and Ahmed whisked through the thick Baobab Forest with catlike elegance that belied the fact assassins were chasing them.

Darts whizzed by their heads with incredible velocity and rapidity. The two young Baol messengers were faster than the Waalo warriors who trailed them by less than 20 meters. Neither Karenga nor Ahmed gave much thought to whether they could outrun the poisoned darts the Waalo blew. The two couriers just ran.

Limbs of trees jutted out. Without losing momentum, the messengers sidestepped the branches that clawed and scratched their flesh.

Ahmed, the faster runner, got the worst of it. His handsome face, marred by several small cuts, contorted. Ahmed lost his balance briefly, seeming to twist his foot on a loose rock. He maintained his lead, though not for long, as he collapsed face-forward on the path. A dart protruded from the left side of his head.

Karenga, an experienced Baol courier, did not lose one stride. Looking straight ahead, he sidestepped Ahmed's arm and dashed past an unseen Alkebulan rock python.

As the forest thinned into brush, Karenga knew he was close to his destination—Lebu'ta. Despite sweaty palms, his firm grip on the wooden cylinder held fast. Karenga could feel the embossed seal press his flesh. The message inside was vital to the success of Nasir Al-Din's jihad. He dared not drop it. He dared not look back at his pursuers or think of poor Ahmed.

The Waalo pursuers blew dart after dart. The constant buzzing past Karenga's ears was akin to a swarm of deadly mosquitoes.

Another pair of poisoned projectiles cut through the air. Karenga felt one brush his cheek. He spied something moving in the distance. *What is it? A Waalo flank? Another enemy?*

Karenga observed Lebu'ta's spectacular waterfall through the spaces between the trees. The breathtaking view, spoiled by the group of warriors closing in on a lone boy, ceased to be his destination. Karenga, Nasir Al-Din's best courier, adeptly changed direction.

The pivot caused Karenga to slow down a tick. More than that, he was suddenly exhausted. His chest heaved before he fell diagonally into the welcoming arms of a baobab tree's limbs. A dart protruded from the nape of his neck.

Within seconds, the assassins swarmed around Karenga's stiffening body. His mind remained alert long enough to feel his pursuers pluck the wooden cylinder from his hand. The small medallion fastened to Karenga's ankle band trembled as a tear slid from his unseeing eye.

The West Alkebulan Waalo vanished into the Baobab Forest on the edge of Lebu'ta.

Chapter 4

The Lamane

The whirling river cascaded over the rocky ledge in an enthusiastic race to the shore. It crashed down the sloped outcrop, churning white from the exertion.

Beneath this waterfall, a solitary boy, Adama, studied the undulating ripples that washed away his footprints. Above him, and as far as his sharp eyes could see, lay his homeland, the ancient nation of Lebu'ta.

Situated south of where the mighty Senegal River empties into the Atlantic Ocean, Lebu'ta enjoyed a sizable coastline. The waterways enriched the nation with good fishing and a robust sea trade. The ocean was visible most days from most vantage points.

The interior was equally striking with a wide variety of tropical flora, fauna, and throngs of valuable baobab trees. Lebu'ta was indeed a beautiful and wondrous place, particularly for a boy of seven.

Adama was too young to know what the coast, nearby islands and peninsula looked like before the insatiable Vumbi raiders weighed anchor. He knew from the royal teacher that the Lebu people, distant relatives of Lebu'ta, had lived peacefully on the peninsula. Then, more than 200 dry seasons ago, the Vumbi raiders, who called themselves Portuguese, arrived, and everything changed. On their heels followed the Dutch and the French.

Adama could speak Portuguese, French, and other Vumbi languages, but did not understand the politics of conquest and enslavement. Like others his age, he was accustomed to the humongous, hideous forts and slave ships that dotted the nation's picturesque seascape. To adults, each structure represented a graphic reminder of coastal threats that attacked Alkebulan's interior in the night, bringing darkness further inland.

Like many nations of West Alkebulan, Lebu'ta was ethnically diverse. Its people spoke various dialects as well as a common language that reflected their Wolof, Lebu, and Serer heritage. Some, like Adama, also spoke Arabic. It was this skill that led Kilifa Ibrahima N'Diaye towards the waterfall in search of his grandson, the prince.

The old man scoured the expanse until he sighted Prince Adama playing under the outcropping. He frowned. The prince was alone, vulnerable, unlike himself who was accompanied by royal warrior-guards. Kilifa inclined his head, and two of the men sprinted towards Adama.

Kilifa held the title of Lamane. As Lamane, he was both king and religious leader of Lebu'ta. Kilifa could serve as Lamane until death unless he voluntarily stepped down or Lebu'tan nobility forced him to abdicate.

Kilifa's family line was long and wide. He could trace his lineage back to the first Wolof king, Burba N'Diadiane N'Diaye. His beloved wife could do likewise. Intermarrying amongst Lebu'tan nobility was commonplace, which led to well-founded distrust. Allegiances shifted unpredictably, and treachery abounded.

Tall, lean and statuesque, the Lamane's dark reddish-brown complexion did not betray his advanced age. Through deep-set eyes, he looked down on his grandson, who knelt before him.

"Maam bu góor," Adama said, "Good Spirit of Lebu'ta. Great Lamane of the land. You are well?"

"Yes, yes, yes. I do not desire a long greeting today. What I desire is obedience. Why are you here alone, grandson? Do you not care for me? Can I bear another loss?"

The Lamane looked at the top of Adama's head, then turned his attention skyward. Massive dark clouds tumbled above the far end of the Baobab Forest, headed towards them. The Lamane's brows knotted as he considered the abrupt change in weather. His thoughts were interrupted by the child's soft voice.

"Djibril threatened to push my face in the dung heap. So, I ran away," Adama said with a furtive peek at his grandfather.

Lamane Kilifa looked down. His scowl softened. "So, you run from the heart of Lebu'ta to the back of Lebu'ta?" the Lamane asked.

"Do you see that trail?" The Lamane pointed towards a beaten path at the mouth of the brush. "That leads to the Baobab Forest. That is a trail of sorrow, Adama. My sorrow.

"You must take off the skin of the gazelle. It has you run from a small insult into the mouth of the cheetah." The Lamane sighed. He placed his hand on the prince's head. The gesture gave Adama permission to rise.

"Get up, boy. I need your help. I have been too long looking for you," Lamane Kilifa said. "Come. We go back with haste. We are too few and too near the Baobab Forest border."

Chapter 5

Adama and Maam bu Góor

Lamane Kilifa stood in front of a drawing of the landmass they called Alkebulan. Near the western shore, lines carved out the borders of Lebu'ta. Unlike some coastal rulers, the Lamane refused to help fill the bellies of the ships as a tactic to avoid raids. But the Vumbi's appetite for flesh grew every dry season, and alliances became more challenging to maintain.

The ever-hostile Waalo pressed the eastern border of Lebu'ta. They had no desire for peace, only more poison for their darts. Although their attacks seemed to lack coordination, the Waalo posed a formidable, bold foe. They were even seen recently in the Baobab Forest.

If the Lamane could get help from Mauritania in the north, he could flank the Waalo with his men in the south and possibly overpower the Sine Kingdom as well. That meant shrewd dealings with Nasir Al-Din, the Mauritanian Berber, who wanted to convert every nation to Islam.

Al-Din vowed to stamp out all Alkebulan rulers who conspired with the Vumbi. The Lamane did not think this was possible, but the Marabout War Al-Din waged had indeed gained momentum.

Lamane Kilifa had dispatched a message to Al-Din, but no reply from the Mauritanian Berber had come.

With hands clasped behind his back, Kilifa turned away from the map. With a confident, commanding voice, he dictated a long, traditional greeting. He looked at his grandson, then continued, "Good spirit Al-Din, we waited long for Karenga and Ahmed. Without hesitation, we consider them dead—your message certainly intercepted."

Adama transcribed each word with careful strokes. The young prince did not pay much attention to the ramifications of what his grandfather was saying. Rather, he entertained himself by translating the words into as many languages as possible, without losing his place. He did this silently in his head. It was similar to a game he used to play with his father, Prince Cheikh Anta.

The Lamane continued speaking, "Treachery abounds on the road from Mauritania. Despite your victory over Jolof, the Waalo do not draw back. Indeed, their darts are sharpened, dipped and flying constantly towards Lebu'ta. The Waalo, like the Kaabu, sell good farmers to the Vumbi." The Lamane paused and looked across the room at his grandson. The scene reminded him of the countless occasions when Prince Cheikh Anta would write his words.

Adama bore little resemblance to his deceased father. The differences ran deeper than the prince's round face and wiry body. Unlike Prince Cheikh Anta, Adama was not aggressive or brave. He would run away to avoid confrontations, much to the Lamane's great shame. But Adama surpassed his father in tongues, spoken and written. The Lamane was very proud of his grandson's skill. If properly developed, it could make Adama more formidable than Cheikh Anta had been.

The Lamane looked out the unglazed window. "The storm has arrived," he murmured, then continued with the letter. "The Vumbi are the most treacherous of all. Even the Waalo dare not get too close to the prison ships."

The high noonday sun became shrouded by massive dark clouds. Rain crashed down on the roof and drowned the Lamane's words.

Lightning struck a nearby baobab tree. Adama only glimpsed the bolt. He stopped writing.

The air seemed to rumble, and the table shifted slightly. Another boom shook the room.

Faster than a Waalo dart, Adama fled the table. He knocked over the stool. Just as he reached his grandfather, the tree creaked, toppled, and came to rest after a tremendous boom. Adama buried his face in his grandfather's cloak.

"It will not do for the next Lamane to fear storms." Lamane Kilifa spoke softly to the young prince. He shifted Adama's face to look outside. Rain came in through the uncovered window and pelted the prince's small head. Adama wanted to free his chin from his grandfather's grip and turn his face away from the storm that raged outside. With all his heart he wanted to, but he did not.

Adama stood beside his grandfather, albeit shaking, blinking his eyes. The child was more afraid of his grandfather's disappointment than the tumult and bright bolts of lightning.

The rain raged. Strong winds pushed through the trees and wailed mournfully. Mesmerized by the scene and the sounds, Adama jumped when his uncle, Mambéty Diop, blew into the room with thunderous expletives.

Chapter 6

Mambéty

Mambéty was soaked from head to foot. Rain dripped from the Vumbi dagger fastened to his waist. Adama abandoned his grandfather's side and ran to embrace his uncle.

"You see I am wet!" Mambéty pushed Adama. The young prince stumbled back into his grandfather, who steadied him. Adama's smile did not waver.

"Where are your manners Mambéty?" Lamane Kilifa eyed his son-in-law sharply. "Your presence is unexpected. You are dripping on my floor," the Lamane gestured at the rainwater pooling under Mambéty's beaded sandals. "You give me no greeting or blessing. Worst of all you shun my grandson who will one day become Lamane!" Kilifa's voice conveyed menace with each increasing decibel.

"Many pardons, father, Good Spirit of Lebu'ta, Great Lamane of the land. I pray for your long life."

The Lamane's face remained as chiseled stone. Adama stepped towards his uncle. The Lamane tightened his grip on the prince's shoulder. Adama winced.

Mambéty glared at the young prince. "Many pardons, nephew. I pray for your prosperity."

Adama beamed and inclined his head towards his uncle in a regal nod.

"And how are my daughter and granddaughter?"

"My beloved wife and our beautiful Awa are well. Never better!" Mambéty's response had a noticeable edge to it.

"Hmm. What has you in such a state Mambéty?"

"The greatest good fortune, Father. I have news from Jean-Claude de Visé." Mambéty's green eyes shone brightly. He absent-mindedly fingered the moss agate stone hilt of his sheathed dagger with one hand and stroked his beard with the other.

"That Vumbi is poison Mambéty. I have told you this. Why do you not take good counsel?" Lamane Kilifa gently guided Adama back to the table. The prince righted the toppled stool and sat down.

Mambéty paced the room. His rain-laden sandals sloshed slightly with each step. He stopped, pivoted, and faced the Lamane.

"Father, we have an opportunity to expand Lebu'ta and destroy our enemies. Jean-Claude will supply new guns and rounds."

"Jean-Claude de Visé is quite benevolent, is he not Adama?"

The prince shrugged. He did not want to oppose his grandfather, and he loved his uncle. Lately the two men were always fighting and Adama was uncertain how to handle the discord. The prince turned his attention back to the letter.

"Yes," the old man rolled the word. "Yet, Jean-Claude speaks not with our elders. He speaks not with me, the Lamane of Lebu'ta. Why is it that this generous Vumbi speaks of the prosperity and safety of Lebu'ta only with you, Mambéty? Do you really believe the benevolent Jean-Claude has only *our* best interests in his heart?"

Mambéty stopped pacing. He averted his green eyes from the Lamane who stared at him intently.

"I beg your pardon, Father. Jean-Claude is certainly in it for the gold, ivory—"

"And the captives! The endless stream of men, women and children marched to the coast who are never seen again. I have heard about the prison ships, Mambéty. The horrors are such I cannot speak it and be clean!"

"They are not Lebu'tan, my father. Trade with Jean-Claude strengthens us and weakens our enemies."

"You are not Lebu—" Lamane Kilifa stopped himself.

Mambéty remained silent, but the nostrils of his long, narrow nose flared. He walked nearer to his nephew and glanced at the letter on the table.

In a quieter tone, the Lamane said, "Are the farmers our enemies, my son? Trade with Jean-Claude? No. No. He is no different than those other Vumbi who came before him. Do you not see how it weakens Lebu'ta and every other Alkebulan nation? This is what you refuse to consume in understanding.

"If things continue, there will be famine in the land. We will not be untouched, Mambéty. We must join Nasir Al-Din's jihad to stop—"

"Al-Din will be crushed!" Mambéty cried, pounding his fist on the table.

Adama jumped at the outburst. The table jolted, and the inkwell toppled. Ink oozed onto the letter Adama had been writing. "Maam bu góor, the letter!" The child quickly righted the bottle and blotted the spilled ink.

Kilifa's eyes flashed hot.

"This is not France Mambéty! First you set aside good manners. Now you dare to raise your voice to me?" His sibilant tone communicated angry disgust. "Am I not the father of your wife? Am I not the great spirit of Lebu'ta? Am I not the Lamane?"

The red undertones of Mambéty's brown skin, still wet from the rainstorm, darkened. Through clenched teeth, he uttered, "Many pardons, Father. I have forgotten my place." There was ice in Mambéty's voice.

Adama thought, *we should crush Lebu'ta's enemies,* even though he did not know who exactly their enemies were.

Mambéty exhaled audibly. "Father Lamane, if we do not negotiate with Jean-Claude others will. Then they will have the guns and the rounds. We do not have the tools necessary to make such weapons. Much of what we have is in disrepair."

"That is because your dear Jean-Claude trades in inferior goods and will not supply what we need to make our own. It is a trick to make us dependent and ill-equipped to fight our true enemy. Our true enemy, Mambéty, is the Vumbi. No matter the language they speak or how they call themselves. We must join with Al-Din or all will be lost."

Adama, who had begun rewriting the letter, looked up at the mention of Al-Din's name.

He must be very important if maam bu góor wants to join with him. But le capitaine Jean-Claude is very important too. Besides, Monsieur le Capitaine gives me sweets from France to eat. Al-Din will not have any of those coming from Mauritania. Just the same old mabuyu baobab chews that we have on celebration days.

"The only answer to the poisonous treachery of the Vumbi is unification," Lamane Kilifa growled with finality. "We must—yes we will—join Nasir Al-Din's jihad!"

Mambéty bent at the waist in a stiff bow of deference to his father-in-law. His downcast eyes resembled cooled lava-like ekanite rather than their usual dark emerald color. He stepped backward, turned, and departed into the raging storm.

Chapter 7

Awa and Mambéty

Awa, age seven, sat on a large, embroidered floor cushion near an open window. She watched sheets of rain move at an angle with great force and speed. The strong winds drove some rain through the window and onto her face. This made Awa look like she was crying, which startled her father when he entered the great room.

"Awa, my dear daughter, what troubles you?" Mambéty's throaty voice was a mix of concern and affection. The princess' solemn, sweet face extinguished the vestiges of anger Mambéty harbored towards the Lamane.

Awa looked up at her father, then placed her slender bejeweled hand on the cover of a large book on her lap. Mambéty's green eyes widened in surprise.

He turned away, shrugged out of his wet cloak, and hung it on a wooden peg. Facing her again, he asked, "What are you doing with that book?"

"Yaye said I was to mend your grand cloak and sent me to fetch it from your inner rooms," she said.

"Yes?"

"I searched and searched. I could not find it."

"Go on," Mambéty urged.

"Then I looked in that old Waalo box you keep in the corner."

"My box?" Mambéty's eyes narrowed.

"Yes, Pape."

"Surely, you are too small to open it," he said. "The top is quite heavy—even for me."

"It is, but I managed to open it."

Mambéty grunted.

Awa continued, "There your cloak lay. When I pulled it out, I heard Uncle Cheikh Anta cry out to me." Awa paused, then said, 'I was afraid. I thought perhaps he wanted to take me with him."

"You do not go with the dead—the dead go with you," Mambéty said flatly.

"Yes, Pape. I remember. And I know Uncle Cheikh Anta would never hurt me. But I was afraid."

Her father nodded his head.

"Then Yaye beckoned me, and I went to her," Awa said. "When she fell asleep, I went back to the room. I went because you and Yaye are brave—I, too, must be brave," Awa said.

A smile passed over Mambéty's lips. He then bade her continue with a flick of his hand.

"I thought Uncle Cheikh Anta's spirit was somehow trapped in the box. I opened the lid and called his name quietly so Yaye would not hear me and wake. Uncle Cheikh Anta did not answer, and I felt foolish.

"I began to pull down the lid when I heard his voice—coming from under your cloaks. Quickly, I removed them.

"He called me until I found his book at the bottom of the box." Awa fell quiet. Her eyes pleaded with her father for answers.

Mambéty looked out the window over Awa's head. "Where is your beloved Yaye?" he asked.

"She is sleeping. You know the rain makes her sleepy," she answered.

Mambéty grunted, then asked, "Did you tell her?"

Awa shook her head.

"Do not tell her," he said softly. "Do not tell anyone. Put the book back."

"Yes, Pape," she said.

"Be sure not to wake your Yaye."

"Yes, Pape."

Mambéty watched Awa stand. Her elegance warmed his heart. *So much like your Yaye*, he reflected.

As she walked, her cowrie shell necklace swayed gently. The movement made the glyph markings on each shell seem animated. The eye-shaped glyph appeared to wink. Mambéty shook his head. *All will be well*, he thought. *All will be well!*

Awa carried the book as if its pages were bound in stone. She walked past Mambéty without engaging his eyes. She stepped behind the wall and out of view.

The princess placed the book beside the large box reverently. She ran her hand over the Waalo carvings that decorated the top of the box and then used both hands to lift the heavy lid. She bent to pick up the book and stopped.

"Awa," cried Uncle Cheikh Anta's disembodied voice. Awa gasped. The cover of the book sprung open.

Back in the great room, Mambéty paced. His wet sandals made ghostly imprints that quickly disappeared. *I did not know Awa's mystic sight was so strong. Such gifts—*The child returned and stood before him, cutting off his thoughts. Mambéty did not seem to notice how sallow her face had become.

"Pape," Awa said, "why do you have Uncle Cheikh Anta's luminosity writings? The book screams out for Good Cousin Adama, my dom ou nijaye, and my betrothed."

"Do not trouble your mind, dear daughter. Many things are beyond your age for understanding. You must trust your Pape."

Mambéty stroked his daughter's hair.

"Pape, I *do* have understanding. Without the book, Uncle cannot live again through Adama. And if Adama does not read the book, he will be cut off from our noble ancestors."

"These things are true. Yes. What is also true is the treachery in Lebu'ta. The book is safe, hidden with me. No one knows it is here, save you.

"Your power is strong. Much more than your beloved Yaye." Mambéty paused, then asked, "What did your uncle say when he cried out to you?"

Awa hesitated, then answered, "He said there is Lebu'tan blood on the Vumbi dagger."

Mambéty looked at his daughter appraisingly. "Speak of this to no one, dear daughter." He reached out, clutched her angular shoulders, and said, "Tell no one. Trust your Pape, and all will be well."

"I will be silent," Awa said. Her father dropped his hands to his sides.

She bowed. Her eyes briefly fixed on the agate stone hilt of Mambéty's dagger. She straightened and stiffly walked away from her father. She sat down on the floor cushion and gazed out the window. A hard wind blew rain through the uncovered opening. It hit her small, upturned face, mixing droplets with tears.

Chapter 8

Souls Depart—Souls Return

ortheasterly winds blew the storm past the heart of Lebu'ta. The hot sun pushed through the remaining clouds and quickly dried the ground.

The majestic blue sky, adorned with bits of orange and yellow reflections from the sun, resembled a Vumbi king's robe. Under this beautiful canopy, the slave ship Liberty weighed anchor. Crewmen hoisted the metal used to moor the vessel to the seabed and stowed it onboard. This final preparation for the voyage complete, the massive vessel slowly headed west from Gorée Island. Its splintered wooden rudder roiled the dead, cold water.

The warped upper deck flooring rattled from the hundreds of human beings straining against chains. From the depths of the hull, mournful wails permeated the acrid air, echoing through cracks and spaces to the fresher air above.

Black-billed seagulls scooped up the sorrowful sounds and took flight inland with the souls of those who had perished. Together they headed back towards the heart of Lebu'ta. The cawing seagulls flew noisily over the heads of the Lebu'tan children and their griot-teacher, the Great Gueweel Gorgui. Everyone looked up at the birds except Awa.

Princess Awa covered her ears with clenched fists. She wanted to drown out the sounds of fear and tremendous sorrow the gulls carried back from the slave ship, Liberty.

Adama shifted his gaze from the birds to his cousin, who seemed to be in pain. He frowned. "What is it Awa?"

She did not respond. Adama grabbed Awa's scrawny shoulder and called her again. She lifted her head and looked at him through wistful, wet eyes.

Awa has not been herself lately, Adama thought. *I hear the elders speak of womenfolk going through ripening. Perhaps that is the trouble.* Coming to that conclusion made Adama feel mature.

"The spirits cry on their way home, and I cry with them," she said.

Adama looked skyward. The flock had all but passed by, save one that swooped down low and showered Gorgui with gull droppings. Adama and the other children, including Awa, who wiped her eyes, laughed. The teacher did not.

Chapter 9

Djibril's Secret

"Pay attention, children! Pay attention, children! I must tell you an important story," Gorgui announced officiously as he cleaned his head with a piece of cloth.

The children settled down. All eyes were on Gorgui. "Ahem!" he cleared his throat for effect, "One day, four children went looking for Lake Retba."

"Why did they go looking for Lake Retba?" Adama asked sarcastically. He giggled and looked over at Awa, who smiled. A small stone hit Adama's ear. "Ow!" he cried.

"Eh, eh!" the griot said. He looked sharply at Adama and then pivoted his gaze to glare at the two boys nearest the prince. The pair, Djibril and his sidekick Samba, snickered until the griot called their names.

The now silent Djibril jutted his chin and fixed his dark eyes upon Adama. When Adama dropped his head, Djibril smirked and thought, *Yes, cousin, I threw the pebble. You can try to make yourself small, but never small enough.*

Djibril, big-boned like his father Moustapha, stood more than three fists taller than Adama. It was hard to believe he and the prince were the same age, and equally difficult to imagine they had been friends.

Everything changed when Uncle Mambéty visited Djibril's father.

Djibril, curious as to why his father would be speaking with Uncle Mambéty, whom his father often spoke ill of, had stood just outside the great room. There, he had overheard bits of words and names spoken quietly by the two men.

Why are they talking about the Lamane, Awa, Adama, and me? Djibril had pondered. *And what animals are they going to capture for this capitaine?*

Djibril had continued to listen. When he heard Uncle Mambéty say clearly that Adama should not—must not—become Lamane, he had become utterly confused. Just then, Djibril's stomach had rumbled heartily. Uncle Mambéty's green eyes had locked on his own.

Trouble, he had thought.

His father had grimaced, then beckoned Djibril into the great room. He had obeyed reluctantly.

"Good Djibril," Uncle Mambéty had said. "It is right that you are listening. These things concern you. Take counsel and heed your elders. It is time for you to put space between yourself and Adama."

It had seemed as if those green eyes were boring a hole into his head. He had looked to his father for answers, for help! But instead his father had nodded and said, "This is my wish."

Djibril had said, "Yes, Pape," but thought, *How can this be? Everyone knows Adama, Samba, Malick, and I play together—always. How can this be right?*

That night, he had asked his father, "Pape, why should Good Cousin Adama not become the great spirit of Lebu'ta?"

His father had responded hushedly, "Good Cousin Adama is not like his father. No, no. The boy is nothing like Cheikh Anta.

"His grandfather believes that when the boy reads Cheikh Anta's luminosity, he will be changed. That is doubtful. Adama is weak and too tender—not like you, son.

"You are like me—big, strong, and unafraid." His father had struck his broad, muscular chest with a closed fist for emphasis. "Mambéty sees these qualities and wants you for his Awa. He works quietly so that you, not Adama, will be the next Lamane."

Moustapha put his hand on Djibril's shoulder and said, "We must each do our part. Do you understand, son?"

"But Adama is my cousin."

"Cousin? We are all cousins. But Adama is not a close cousin to you like a dom ou badjeen, son of my sister, or a dom ou nijaye, son of my brother. So do as I say."

"Yes, Pape." Djibril's eyes had filled with tears.

"Good. Speak of this to no one, or we may all cease speaking, and our blood will be lost."

Chapter 10

Gueweel Griot Gorgui

Adama knew Djibril had thrown the pebble—the only child who would dare do so.

What have I done to Djibril that he hates me so?

The prince's thought quickly skipped over the unanswered question to the memory of Djibril pushing him down. Adama could still feel the eyes of all the children who stopped playing to gawk at him. He could sense Djibril's eyes on him now as they sat waiting for the griot to begin again.

The prince kept his head down and put his elbows on his crossed legs. His musing turned to the dim memory of his father, Cheikh Anta.

The elders said Cheikh Anta, wise, cunning and strong, would have been a uniting force in Alkebulan. But the younger men told of Cheikh Anta's fighting skills. His father had often bested the great Moustapha. Those were the stories the prince liked best.

Adama wished he could read his father's luminosity writings and gain the courage to pound his tormenter into dust. *It's just a matter of time,* Adama thought, *before I crush you.*

"Ah ah," Gorgui uttered his habitual guttural interjection, which penetrated Adama's dark reverie.

The griot said, "Now, no more interruptions. You must have respect for your elders and for our stories. I am an elder who knows the stories, so I must get twice as much respect."

A small man, Gorgui's weathered skin looked stretched on his narrow-elongated face. In many ways, Gorgui resembled a giant eland antelope. His long hair, parted down the center, was tightly wound into braids resembling large spiraled horns. The plaits made his head, which contained a wealth of information, seem enormous.

Like the alpha eland male, whose horns enforce dominance over the herd, Gorgui used his vast knowledge strategically. Gorgui schemed and, when necessary, shifted alliances. Although an outsider who came from far beyond the Baobab Forest, he bested his peers in every area. Thus, he earned the title of Great Gueweel, an honor usually held exclusively by Lebu'tan and Wolof griots. He, and he alone, had use of the ancient teaching seat—a resined chair hewn from a large tree stump.

As the teacher of the royal children, Gorgui was able to shape the minds of future leaders. Through the children, he also learned about private matters and schisms within the nobility. That is how the great teacher knew about the uneasy alliance between Awa's father, Mambéty, and Djibril's father, Moustapha.

Gorgui understood both Mambéty and Moustapha's opposition to the aging Lamane Kilifa's push for Adama to rule Lebu'ta and wed Awa. Mambéty made it clear to the griot that Djibril was preferable as both ruler and son-in-law. Gorgui assessed Djibril as being slow-witted and pliable. Such a combination could allow Mambéty to be the true Lamane.

But what of Moustapha? Mambéty made it known to Gorgui that he felt Moustapha, though physically imposing, could be easily controlled—or removed. But Gorgui did not share this opinion. The griot doubted Moustapha would let Mambéty make a fool of his son Djibril. He had told Mambéty this.

Gorgui did not dislike Moustapha but preferred Mambéty. He thought it more likely that Mambéty would come to control Lebu'ta, and he, Gorgui, would be his advisor. Assuming Lamane Kilifa did not kill them all first.

Chapter 11

A Lebu'tan Story

The royal children sat quietly under the hot noonday sun. Each pair of clear eyes looked expectantly at the great griot Gorgui. The teacher relished the attention and the respect he commanded. His nostrils swelled with pride as he reassessed his audience.

There was Adama, the heir apparent to Lamane Kilifa. Awa, Adama's betrothed, and their second cousin, Djibril. The other Lebu'tan noble children sat interspersed, including Samba, Malick, Khadija, and Yacine.

Gorgui eyed each child in turn with his death stare. It was effective. The griot expected no more interruptions. He continued with the lesson.

"One day, four children went looking for Lake Retba," Gorgui said. The griot paused, then asked, "Why did the children go looking for Lake Retba?" Gorgui made eye contact with Adama, who shrugged and lowered his eyes.

The griot continued, "Because they wanted to see, for themselves, if the water was truly pink. Ah ah.

"Like the great gueweel griots of the Wolof Empire, I have seen

Lake Retba. Yes, I have seen and tasted it. I tell you it is very pink and very salty.

"But the children, who went looking for Lake Retba, did not ask me. No, not one of the four," he paused for effect. "So, they walked a long way, in the wrong direction, and never did find it."

Adama and the other children laughed. A master storyteller, Gorgui waited a moment before speaking.

"It is always best to seek advice from an elder. Why?"

"It keeps the spirit humble and the body alive," a few children replied.

"Correct. This is something every child should know. But these children did not respect the ways of Lebu'ta. We will see what happened to them. Ah ah.

"The sun had gone down, and the moon did not shine. They lost their way. None saw the bukki hyena hiding behind a baobab tree's stout trunk. You all know the bukki are cunning, dangerous animals."

"Yes," all the children said.

"The bukki crept out and began walking alongside the children. Bukki greeted them as if he were their friend."

Gorgui, dramatizing the hyena, lowered the timbre of his voice and asked, "Who do you children belong to?

"One boy answered, saying he belonged to our merciful Roog. Another answered that he belonged to our spiritual interceders, Pangool. The next child answered he belonged to our divine spirit Takhar. The last boy hesitated, his thoughts dulled by fear, then said that he belonged to bukki!"

There was a collective gasp from the boys and girls. Satisfied, the griot continued.

"Bukki thought for a moment, then said to the first boy, 'Roog Sene is our creator god. You are well protected.'

"To the second, he said, 'Pangool are the spirits of our ancestors. You are well protected.'

"To the third child, he said, 'Takhar is our god of justice and vengeance. You are well protected.'

"To the last boy, he said, 'I will eat you. Then you will be with me at all times and very well protected indeed!'"

The griot laughed and broke the spell. "Ah, ah. You see, nothing good happens when the young veer from the ways of their ancestors.

"Alkebulan is vast and full of dangers," Gorgui said. "Take this counsel," his voice became somber, "keep Lebu'ta in your heart wherever you may travel."

Gorgui looked over the tops of the children's heads. His gaze fell on a powerfully built man standing off to the side. The man beckoned. The griot observed the summons. One of his many braids fell across his face. Gorgui smiled as he pushed the coiled lock back in place with a shaky hand. He looked back at the children who sat expectantly.

"Enough. Yes, one story is enough for today. Go and learn from your elders so Lebu'ta may continue in prosperity and safety. Go!"

He shooed them away and ambled over to the man who waited.

Chapter 12

Gorgui and Moustapha

Moustapha stepped off the path and into the brush he hoped concealed him. There he stood watching Gorgui, his son, Djibril, and the other children. Finally, the griot hastened towards him. "Greetings, honorable Moustapha. I pray for your long life and prosperity," Gorgui said. The words oozed out.

"Great Gorgui, caretaker of all Lebu'tan folktales, history, and genealogies. I pray likewise for your prosperity," Moustapha replied. Then, through his bared, thick white teeth, he said, "The length of your life may well be shortened if deceptions become known to me."

The griot said, "I am but a humble servant to the Lamane, you, and all Lebu'ta." He bowed deeply. "I do not forget my place, Good Moustapha."

Much to Moustapha's annoyance, Gorgui did not rattle easily. *But*, he thought, *what good is a faint-hearted counselor?*

"Griot, I did not come to trade empty words," Moustapha said. He surveyed his surroundings with quick, furtive movements. No one was walking on the path or in the brush behind them. The children remained within his eyesight yet beyond earshot.

"What of Mambéty's plan? Eh? A box with danger on all sides."

"Yes, there is much danger," Gorgui said. "But I see no way but for you to move forward."

"Mambéty is correct. We need Vumbi weapons. If we do not move now, Lebu'ta will soon become weak and fall."

"Ah ah. Your answer comes from your own lips," Gorgui said slyly.

"You play all sides in this box." Moustapha cut his eyes at the griot, then asked, "Does the Lamane have reason to act against Mambéty? Does he suspect?"

Gorgui took a moment before answering, "I do not believe the Lamane has plans against his daughter's husband."

Moustapha grunted. He looked over at the children and asked, "What is your opinion of Adama?"

The griot dipped his head. "Adama is young and has much to learn, as do the other boys."

"You tell me what I see with my eyes. Do not trifle with me, griot. I know you conspire with Mambéty to elevate my son."

Gorgui's nose twitched.

"Eh! I see from your face I am correct. You two think I am without wisdom, and Mambéty will rule Lebu'ta through my son."

Gorgui gestured with his palms up.

"Am I to stand aside? Or do you think I can be cast aside?" Moustapha asked.

Both men knew Mambéty—shrewd and ruthless as a bukki— could very well outmaneuver the Lamane. Yes, Mambéty could have Djibril, rather than Adama, ascend as successor. But the cost would be high.

"I serve the Good Spirit of Lebu'ta, the Great Lamane of the land, faithfully. But the Lamane's great affection for Adama is no secret.

"He wishes Adama to wed Awa and rule as Lamane. How can Djibril find favor?" The wary griot spoke carefully. He said no words Moustapha could carry to the Lamane and betray him.

"I do not dislike the boy," mused Moustapha. "How can I when he looks so much like his yaye?"

"You were very fond of his yaye, yes?"

"That is not your concern, griot!" Moustapha all but spat the last word. He would not address the griot as the Great Gueweel Gorgui—just griot. It was Moustapha's way of reminding Gorgui of his status. Gorgui, like Mambéty, was an honorary Lebu'tan whose lineage hailed from beyond the Baobab Forest.

Gorgui pulled his lips back in what looked like a smile. Moustapha's arm shot out. He grabbed the griot's neck and growled.

"You have no loyalty to Lebu'ta. It is clear your allegiance is to Mambéty.

"Hear me, griot, I will not step aside, and I will not be pushed. This will not be. This will not be!

"Take care with the games you play with Kilifa—and me."

Chapter 13

The Challenge

The children scrambled to their feet. The boys drifted to one side and the girls to the other. Awa, Khadija, and Yacine chatted affably. Adama and his friend Malick laughed whilst his tormentor Djibril spoke with Samba. Adama had a true friend in Malick. The boy did not hold grudges. He seemed to understand Adama's fears and weaknesses.

The Good Malick always helped and advised Adama, though often in vain because Adama rarely took heed. Perhaps it was Malick's dislike for Djibril and that warthog Samba. Perhaps it was his father's teaching to never let any man rule him through fear or kindness. Whatever the reason, Malick stood up for Adama more often than not.

"Hey Adama, we are going to Lake Retba. You and Malick coming?" Djibril asked.

Adama shot Malick a frightened look, which his friend mirrored. All children knew they were not to leave Lebu'ta—it was forbidden.

"You know we are not to leave Lebu'ta without an elder," said Malick.

"Ach! That is for little boys. You two are little, little boys," retorted Djibril.

"Yeah, you stay here and play with the little girls and learn to cook," Samba added, laughing.

Djibril laughed too. Malick and Adama exchanged apprehensive glances.

Awa and her friends tuned in to the banter. Yacine, pretty and plump, shouted, "If women did not cook, men would not eat, and boys are like scraps anyway!" The girls giggled.

Addressing Adama, Awa said in a monotone voice, "You must not leave Lebu'ta. You will not return."

Adama shivered.

"Aw, you do not know. You do not have the far-seeing eyes of your yaye," Djibril taunted.

"She does too," Yacine said.

"Yes, Awa is a great seer. You are the one who does not know Djibril. You are fat and stupid!" Malick yelled.

Djibril socked Malick on the side of the head. The boy stumbled back and fell on his bottom. Quickly, Djibril bounded over Malick's outstretched legs, his fists poised to strike. He landed with a thud just an arm's length away from the prince. Adama's eyes locked on Djibril's, who advanced towards him. Adama's eyes grew wide before he turned and ran. Djibril did not pursue Adama. Rather, he laughed, and Samba joined in. Their chorus of laughter slapped Adama's ears and spurred him to run faster. He did not see Malick spring up and jump on Djibril or Yacine cuff Samba on the jaw.

Moustapha and Gorgui observed the incident with grim faces. Lamane Kilifa, standing far off, was close enough to witness his grandson's actions and Moustapha's conversation with Gorgui.

Chapter 14

Capitaine Jean-Claude de Visé

The master of the French ship, Le Bon Dieu, watched distractedly as a small lifeless body was cast over the side. He said no prayer for the soul of the child who had served him. Indeed, le capitaine had walked away before the shroudless corpse tumbled into the water.

On the long journey from Nantes to Gorée, the cabin boy had been about as useful as a barnacle. The child blundered even the simplest errand. Of course, the gold livres the boy's aunt had paid Capitaine Jean-Claude de Visé were generous. The shimmer of the coins undoubtedly prompted le capitaine to promise the credulous woman he would apprentice the stupid child. Well, the boy was dead, and that was lesson enough.

Jean-Claude had made four previous trips to the westernmost area of the continent, which the locals called Alkebulan. On each voyage, he anchored at Gorée—for good reason. Gorée was a French settlement, complete with a fort. It existed with the permission of the local nobility, who received goodly tributes in return.

Tributes ensured trade remained orderly and profitable. Privateers, like Jean-Claude, could concentrate on repairing their vessels, stocking supplies, and acquiring humans.

Le Bon Dieu, safely anchored, required only minor fixes. Jean-Claude did not concern himself with the details. The crew would see to it. The privateer brooded over how to stretch the remaining livres. Food for both men and captives could be costly. Hungry sailors became mutinous, and slaves, dead from starvation, had no value.

The trip to Saint Lucia could take weeks or months. *Ah! If but God would see to strong winds*, Jean-Claude thought, *and enough food.*

Preoccupied, le capitaine did not hear the coxswain address him. The old salt tapped him on the shoulder, and Jean-Claude spun round. His long, greasy hair, tied with a leather strip, bobbed like the tail of a frightened horse.

"Pardon, mon capitaine," the coxswain said.

"Oui?"

"Monsieur Badjan," he answered, gesturing to a short, very dark man with straight golden hair. Badjan, a Métis merchant of ill repute, smiled. Jean-Claude's green eyes twinkled. "Bonjour mon amie Badjan," he said.

I am saved, Jean-Claude thought. *This is why I anchor at Gorée. These mixed-race Métis have the cunning of the Waalo and the morals of the French. And the women—ah, the Signares! C'est magnifique. Such beauty, nowhere else. Ah, ha, ha, Signare Maguette, I will see you soon.*

Jean-Claude's reverie was short-lived. Badjan's smile widened into a nasty grin. Jean-Claude's face reddened. "Come. Let me see if your prices are worth my time. I have much to do."

Chapter 15

Troubled Waters

ean-Claude walked to the bulwark of Le Bon Dieu. His knee-length cracked leather boots gently squeezed his swollen legs. He ignored the throbbing in his calf as he gulped putrid sea air and looked at the vast ocean.

Le capitaine had bargained deftly with the Métis pig, Badjan. He smiled. At that moment, the Liberty, a British competitor vessel, floated into his line of vision. He watched it impassively.

As the Liberty approached the horizon, Jean-Claude noted its balloon-like hull sagged in the water. He surmised the ship bore too heavy a load.

The Liberty, a fluyt ship like Le Bon Dieu, had three masts and a vast cargo hold. A Dutch invention, fluyts required few crewmen and thus were relatively inexpensive to operate.

Jean-Claude observed the violent agitation of the Liberty's white sails. Without looking up, he knew the canvas above his head only fluttered softly. Leaning forward a bit, Jean-Claude narrowed his green eyes. *Was that smoke wafting or just the movement of the sails?* He pulled out the brass telescope given to him by his maternal grandfather, a Dutch privateer, and peered. With the aid of the lens, he could see the flames shooting up from the deck.

"Sacrebleu!" Jean-Claude closed the three-draw telescope, made the sign of the cross, kissed his fingers, and frowned. *Pirates? Dutch Privateers? Mutiny? Rebellion?* The possibilities tripped over each other in his mind.

Jean-Claude blew a deep breath through slightly parted lips. It did not matter what caused Liberty's calamity. He could not afford such misfortune.

Le Bon Dieu was a new construction. A fine ship, lightly armed with only a single cannon. Jean-Claude had commissioned the Dutch vessel two years earlier. He ran into trouble paying for it and had to do without the second cannon and optional comforts. This was Le Bon Dieu's maiden voyage, and it had to make enough money to pay past due debts.

As he gazed at the spot where the fireball that was the Liberty dissolved into the horizon, Jean-Claude contemplated his trip back to France by way of Saint Lucia. He had to barter with Mambéty deftly. The firearms, liquor, and other goods he brought for bartering had to stretch. It had to be enough.

Jean-Claude wanted at least 100 men, women, and children to enslave, as well as gold ore, ivory, and other desirable commodities. The slaves that survived the voyage would be delivered to Saint Lucia. He should get at least 60 livre per head for fit adults and a thousand livre for children.

Jean-Claude knew that anywhere from 15 to 20 percent of the people transported across the Atlantic Ocean died during the long crossing. He mulled over the calculations in his head.

I must have no fewer than 40 children. This way, I will have at least 32 to sell. I will pay the crew, the Dutch shipbuilder and have enough for my next trip. Next time, I will hire a ship's doctor and increase the number of slaves I can sell.

This is a good plan. Sound. Mambéty must deliver on his promise. He must keep me, keep us, from disaster.

A planter on Saint Lucia hired Le Bon Dieu to transport sugar off the island. The sugar and non-human merchandise from Alkebulan—gold ore, beeswax, gum arabic—would return with him to Nantes. All would sell quickly and profitably.

Laughter from his hired crew pierced Jean-Claude's thoughts. He turned away from the bulwark.

"You," Jean-Claude barked, pointing at a red-faced, portly crewman. "Yes, you," he said, almost sweetly, then growled, "Sacrebleu! You son of a bilge rat!" Le capitaine's anger choked every crewman's throat into silence. "There is much work to be done. I am not paying for frivolity. Step lively. Step lively! All of you scoundrels, step lively, I say!"

The crewman scurried out of sight. The clang of leg irons and chains they carried in preparation for the human captives rattled as they fled below deck. A miniature pair, the right size for a small child, slipped out of a sailor's hand and into a bucket of filth.

Part Three

Lake Retba

"When I discover who I am, I'll be free."

—Ralph Ellison

Chapter 16

Kilifa's Posterity

The long, thick stone wall of Lebu'ta stood as high as the gigantic wall of Kano in the Hausa Kingdom. Lamane Kilifa had visited Kano once as a boy. But that wall did not have the beautiful ancient glyphs he now gazed upon in the expansive royal garden.

The sacred symbols, carved in rows and columns, told the story of Lebu'ta. How the people traveled from Kemet in the far northeast, settling first in Mali before continuing towards the Atlantic.

Lamane Kilifa gazed up at the colossal wall. He drank in its solid magnificence. It had been there from the beginning. He wondered if it would remain until the end.

The late afternoon sun slashed the stone with violet strokes, making it look cut and bruised. Kilifa placed his hand between glyphs. He thought about his triple obligations, to the ancestors, to the living, and to those yet to be born.

Sighing deeply, Lamane Kilifa, direct descendant of the Burba N'Diadiane N'Diaye, turned his attention to his only grandson and asked, "What happened today with Good Malick?" The ruler's soft voice sounded weary with disappointment.

With downcast eyes, Adama frowned and shrugged.

"Adama, look at me," the Lamane said. He repeated his question more firmly, "What happened today with Malick?"

"Malick stood up to Djibril for Awa. Djibril hit him and knocked him down," the prince replied.

"Ah! Malick is Awa's friend, and he defended her. Malick is your friend too, is he not?"

The prince nodded.

"Awa is your friend and your betrothed, is she not?"

The prince nodded again.

"So why did you run away?"

Adama shrugged.

The Lamane caressed his grandson's cheek and lifted his head. "Running away from your problems will not do."

"Djibril is much bigger than me. I was afraid," Adama whispered.

"What is the worst Djibril could have done to you? Hmm?"

"He could have knocked me down like he did Malick. Kicked me and punched me," the child said. Then he continued in an excited voice, "And, and, and, he might even have killed me!"

"Only the body dies, Adama, not the spirit. Your father's spirit is not dead, is it?"

Adama shook his head.

"No. It is here," Lamane Kilifa said, making an all-encompassing gesture. "It is here," he pointed at his grandson's chest. "It is everywhere. And he would have helped you defeat Djibril today if you had called on him. You must use the strength of our ancestors' spirits."

"Is that the luminosity maam bu góor? May I read my father's luminosity?" Adama's face brightened.

The Lamane smiled, "No. You are not ready to read your father's luminosity."

The prince frowned and dropped his head.

"But I think you are ready to learn how to *write* the luminosity. What do you think?"

"Yeah!" Adama exclaimed. "I am ready maam bu góor."

"Good. Go get Awa, and we will begin." The Lamane frowned as he watched his grandson run. The young prince yelled, "Awa! Awa!"

Kilifa's eyes grew gray and wistful. He loved his grandson dearly. But the boy was so fragile. So different from the Lamane's son, whom he missed deeply. There was nothing Kilifa could not tell Cheikh Anta, even when his son was Adama's age.

Ah! How can I tell Adama that Cheikh Anta's luminosity writing is lost? He is not ready for that truth. No, he is not. But soon, the day may come when I cannot protect him from the truth.

The Great Lamane turned his eyes towards the ancient wall. Slowly, he moved away from his gloomy thoughts and towards the glyph carvings.

He ran a slender finger over a chiseled double oval. The symbol meant Lebu'ta and eternity.

Lebu'ta will always be. It must!

Chapter 17

Secret Writing

Ta, toe, ta, tam.

The skin of a djembe drum cried out, fell silent, then cried out again in a less-than-perfect replica. One of the children was learning to play. The light breeze carried the sounds of the child's potential to the keen ears of Kilifa, the Great Lamane of Lebu'ta.

Straight-backed and regal, the Lamane paced the grounds of the royal garden as he awaited his own pupils. Finally, he heard voices over the sounds of the drum. The banter between his grandchildren and his personal guards brought a faint smile to his stoic face.

When the prince and princess burst into view, the Lamane's smile widened briefly, flattened, then disappeared. In a leg race, the children ran towards him with abandon. He regarded them appraisingly. *A good day for teaching,* he thought. *But how much to give?* He glanced at the metal ceremonial bowl near the wall.

Awa reached the Lamane first, kneeled, then said, "Good spirit of Lebu'ta." She bowed her head. "You are well?"

Adama fell to his knees and said, "Great Lamane of the land." He, too, lowered his head. "You are well?"

"Yes, yes. I am well," Lamane Kilifa replied, then placed a hand on each child's head. "Sit—you have much to learn today."

Gracefully, Awa lowered herself backward onto the grass. Adama sat back on his heels beside her.

The Lamane took several short steps to and fro, then stood in front of the prince and said, "It is time, Adama. You must prepare to take your place as my successor...with your betrothed, Awa.

"The N'Diaye tree has many branches. We have always been the strongest and closest to the mighty Burba N'Diadiane.

"But many twigs desire to be Lamane. That must not be. We are N'Diaye! You must prepare to take your rightful place.

"It has been almost two dry seasons since your father, the Great Prince Cheikh Anta, was killed."

"How did my uncle die?" the princess asked quietly.

The Lamane did not answer.

Adama cast his eyes downward. "Please, maam bu góor. No one ever speaks of my pape's death," said the prince. "They say he was a great man, and that is all."

After a long pause, the Lamane said, "I am pained to do so."

"Please," Awa pleaded.

He regarded his grandchildren, inhaled deeply, then, with resignation, said, "As you wish.

"Do you know what slave raids are?"

The children nodded their heads.

"They are a plague worse than locusts. Slave raids weaken Lebu'ta—all Alkebulan.

"It has gone on for too long. For generations, the Vumbi have watered the land with distrust and have harvested Alkebulan bodies from greedy kings."

"Why are the Vumbi hungry for bodies?" Adama asked.

"Why? I do not know. No matter their language, the Vumbi are as hawks, eagles, and owls fighting over prey that yet lives."

Looking at Awa, the Lamane added, "Mambéty does not see that our only hope is to join with other Alkebulan nations and kingdoms to fight the Vumbi, the Waalo, and all those who aid them."

The Lamane patted her head and continued. "Good spirit Nasir Al-Din, the Mauritanian Marabout, understood this wisdom.

"Quietly, he had summoned peaceful kingdoms, Lebu'ta and a few other nations to Lake Retba. He used his best couriers, Karenga and Ahmed, to ensure secrecy.

"When we received Al-Din's message, Griot Gorgui had counseled me to send Cheikh Anta and Mambéty. I agreed—*we all agreed*. I sent a few soldiers with them for protection. Would I had known! I would have sent all of Lebu'ta, for there was treachery awaiting my son.

"On the path home, through the Baobab Forest, they were ambushed by Waalo assassins.

"Mambéty, badly wounded in the fight, managed to get Cheikh Anta back to Lebu'ta—but not alive."

"And my yaye?" Adama asked.

"Your yaye? There is little I can tell.

"We awaited Cheikh Anta and Mambéty's return. The sun had begun to move past the edge of the sea...the meeting had surely ended. Your maam bu jigéen became sick with worry.

"Later, I learned the royal guards saw your yaye afar off running alone towards the Baobab Forest. They pursued her as fast as they could.

"When the guards entered the forest, they only found Mambéty carrying Cheikh Anta. Mambéty said he had not seen your yaye on the path home.

"The guards and soldiers searched and searched the forest. We know not what happened to her. "

"Is she dead?" Adama whispered the question.

"Perhaps." The Lamane looked at the tears falling from his grandchildren's eyes and said, "But the human essence does not die. Dry your eyes."

Adama and Awa wiped their eyes and rubbed their cheeks.

"Do not cry. If she is dead, she is united with beloved Cheikh Anta and has become an ancestor.

"And you both know ancestors live with us as spirits, yes?"

The children nodded their heads.

"Good. Pay attention and take this knowledge from me. The luminosity is a different way—a special way—our ancestors live with us and *through us*. Only certain Lebu'tans have the skill and the gift of luminosity."

Speaking to Awa, Lamane Kilifa said, "It is similar to the mystic gift of sight your yaye has, and *you have*. Similar, but not the same. Your gift of sight lets you see that part of the future our merciful Roog will *let* you see."

The Lamane bid his grandchildren rise and led them closer to the glyph-carved wall. "Go, gather some baobab twigs. We must make a fire." He sat on a stone stool. The children ran off. Kilifa relaxed and allowed his shoulders to sag for a moment.

Within a few minutes, they returned and stood before him with several twigs in their hands. "Place the twigs in a pile," the Lamane said, pointing to the place on the ground near a metal bowl.

"Now, start a fire as I showed you, Adama. Do not use all of the twigs." Turning to the princess, he said, "Go find some beetles. Be quick!" Awa obeyed.

When the princess returned, the Lamane motioned for her to sit on the ground beside Adama. "Put the beetles in the bowl and kill them with those twigs," he said, pointing. She did so. "Good. Now, we must wait for the fire to die."

After the small fire died, Lamane Kilifa led his grandchildren in a prayer.

Great Creator, reveal the secrets of this writing to my descendants so that I live. Let the luminosity unite our minds and double our strength.

"We must cool the ashes whilst the prayer is on our breath," the

Lamane said as he blew on the ashes. The children followed suit, blowing loudly.

"Good," the Lamane said. "Now put the soot on top of the beetles and crush them together with the twigs." Adama took the lead and jabbed at the insects and burnt twigs.

"You too, Awa," the Lamane urged his granddaughter. The princess joined in.

"Good. This mixture serves as the ink. To write with it, you will need to make a brush. A special brush made from the hair of a person you love."

The children giggled.

"Oh yes. A luminosity writing requires it."

"Grandfather, why does Adama get to write and I do not?" asked Awa.

"Ah! In Lebu'ta, there are two things women do, besides bear children, that men cannot. They can see sickness before the body falls ill. And through their dreams, our women pierce the veil of time to see things yet to come. Special women, like your yaye," he said, smiling at Awa, "also see whilst awake."

"My yaye used to see things too," said Adama.

"Yes, she did," agreed the Lamane. "Yes, she did," he repeated and paused. He seemed far away for a moment, then abruptly cleared his throat. "Sovereign men of Lebu'ta use luminosity writing to pass down their essence, which their descendants pull forward."

The children uttered sounds of wonderment.

"Yes. More than a thousand dry seasons ago, our women had a form of luminosity writing. But the art was lost when the Hellenic Vumbi invaded Kemet. Much was lost when we fled northeastern Alkebulan. Yet, much was gained when we settled in Lebu'ta.

"Enough. We will end your lesson here because the writing must take place at dawn. As the sun lifts its head over the horizon," the Lamane pointed towards the sea, "the writer must ask his soul to speak the truth to his spirit.

"When the sun strikes his face at sunrise, he must write what he overheard his soul say."

"What if he does not hear anything?" Adama asked.

"He will hear because this is how he will live again to fulfill his purpose."

"What if he does not have a purpose?" the prince inquired.

"Everyone has a purpose," Awa said softly.

"Yes, each of us has a purpose. The luminosity writing breathes life into words so they can be inhaled by descendants who continue the purpose. The luminosity carries the past into the present and provides knowledge and strength."

"But how, grandfather, I do not understand?" Adama whined.

"Ah, Adama, I think it is too high for you to understand now."

"But I want to understand so I may read my father's luminosity and become strong and brave just like he was."

"Be patient. It is not time for that yet, Adama. Remember, the luminosity, like everything else, is paired. There is day, there is night. There is boy, there is girl. With the luminosity, there is writing, and there is reading. I have shown most of the steps to the writing. But the reading cannot be shown. The reading is experienced.

"The reading is...*well*, it is difficult to describe.

"When I read my father's luminosity, my eyes loosened his written words. Those words were pulled by my mind," the Lamane said whilst gesturing towards his forehead. "I felt them enter my very soul through my nostrils. When I finished, my father *and* our ancestors were alive again—*within me*—as part of my very soul!"

"Woah!" the children exclaimed. "How maam bu góor? Tell us." The pair looked at him expectantly.

But the Lamane shook his head. "That is all for today, children. I am weary." His tone was firm. "Be sure to visit your maam bu jigéen. I saw her making mabuyu baobab chews."

"Ooh! Her baobab chews are the best in Lebu'ta," Awa said.

The children bid their grandfather departing blessings and withdrew.

When the prince and princess were out of view, Kilifa, the Great Lamane of Lebu'ta, seemed diminished. He buried his face, sorrow, and shame in the crook of his arm. Tears fell onto his royal cloak. He wept silently but without restraint.

Chapter 18

Conspiring Cousins

Mambéty's hand guided the dagger around the edge of the embossed tube. The gap it created was just enough to wedge the flat edge of the blade in between and force the prize open. His fingers poked along the interior edge of the wooden cylinder.

"Ah ha!" He plucked a tightly rolled paper from within. The tube slipped from his hand and hit tightly packed earth. It rocked slightly, then settled near Vumbi-made boots.

The thick-soled boots made Jean-Claude's long walk through the Baobab Forest easier. But they did not prevent the privateer from feeling the tube he trod upon when he hastened to see the epistle in Mambéty's hands.

Two sets of green eyes peered at the written words.

"What does it say, cousin Mambéty?" asked Jean-Claude.

Although their blood bond was Dutch, the two men spoke in French. Jean-Claude's Lebu'tan was much worse than Mambéty's French, and neither man's Dutch was very good.

"Je ne sais pas. It is Arabic, I think," said Mambéty.

"Ah, yes. Nasir Al-Din would write in Arabic," said Jean-Claude. "We must know what it says.

"Badjan told me the true menace is Al-Din's war chief, Sidy. He said Sidy is like the devil—everywhere at once. Quel désastre!" Jean-Claude strode a few paces away from his cousin, then turned towards him. "I sail in three days. I can ill afford any interference from Sidy or anyone else. Nor can you, Mambéty. Nor can you!"

Jean-Claude kicked the partially buried tube. It bounced off a rock and rolled back to Mambéty's elegantly sandaled foot.

Mambéty stooped and picked it up. Squeezing it tightly, he said, "I will use the boy. Damn, his grandfather's protection!"

The two men nodded in agreement. In Dutch, they said, "Nothing is better than a grandfather's love," and laughed.

The saying, a favorite of their grandfather, Kapitein Pieter Schouten, was almost all the Dutch either knew. As children, they vied for the affection of the man they called Opa Pieter. As men, Opa Pieter was an achievement marker to surpass—each intent on doing so, with or without the other.

Their laughter faded into reveries. The two men made their way out of the clearing and into the Baobab Forest's dense growth. *Mambéty's chortle has not changed much from when we first met,* thought Jean-Claude as they walked.

The privateer recalled the one and only voyage he had made with their grandfather. So long ago, yet so vivid in his mind.

Perhaps he remembered because that crossing, long and hard, taught him the kindness and the cruelty of the sea. More likely, it was because that's when Jean-Claude learned Opa Pieter was a pirate.

Chapter 19

Jealous Nostalgia

"Oui" Jean-Claude said. He followed close behind Mambéty, who led their trek through dense growth. His cousin protectively held back most of the thorny branches, but some broke free and whipped le capitaine about the head and shoulders.

Jean-Claude dodged a thick limb and clambered over a massive baobab root. "Your laughter reminds me of the past," he said. "Ah. You sound much like Opa Pieter, cousin Mambéty."

"Perhaps," replied Mambéty. "But you are more like him. You are a most competent capitaine, cousin, just as he was. And you chose a woman for her money, not for love. The money you spent, but you still have the shipyard."

But Opa did marry for love, Jean-Claude thought. *He loved your grandmother. Even though she was Waalo—albeit a Métis—he married her first. Your mother was born before my mother. And you are older than I. Yes, dear cousin, all of you came first, leaving little for us.*

Jean-Claude closed his mind to the bitterness and said, "Who could love such a one as I married? She fusses all day and snores all night. Agh!"

Mambéty laughed, and this time, Jean-Claude laughed also. The two men strode out of the thicket and onto a well-trodden footpath. They continued their trek side-by-side.

"So, you have said many times. I am very fortunate. My wife is very pretty, and our daughter is a delight," Mambéty said.

"Ah! *All* of the men in Lebu'ta are fortunate. The most beautiful women in the world are in Lebu'ta." *Hmm,* he thought, *even your Awa is prettier than my petite Madeleine.*

"They cook well too—not better than my maam bu jigéen and yaye—but good." Mambéty conceded.

Jean-Claude knew his companion spoke of his grandmother and mother. "I remember your grandmother's food," he said, then complimented, "C'était magnifique! And the sweets. Ah! No better baobab chews and mabuyu in the world!"

Mambéty nodded his head. "Not even my yaye could cook as well as my maam bu jigéen."

The cousins walked in companionable silence. Mambéty's light footfalls contrasted with Jean-Claude's heavy steps and rumbling belly.

"My stomach, too, reminisces. It thinks of my wife's cooking, not her face." Jean-Claude laughed. "Of course, many Frenchmen marry homely women who satisfy their appetites...and find beauté outside the home to satisfy their hearts," Jean-Claude added knowingly.

"Do you speak of your beloved, Signare Maguette?" asked Mambéty. "You will see her before you depart?"

"Oui. I suppose I will have a little time to pay my respects to the Métis beauté."

"So nonchalant cousin?" Mambéty eyed Jean-Claude shrewdly.

"Meh,"

"Meh? No, no. The fiery Signare Maguette is more than enough to satisfy the yearnings of any man. Confine your passions to her house."

Jean-Claude did not respond.

Mambéty's nose flared. "Women have always been your weakness. Your impetuous desires have gotten us into—"

"S'il vous plaît!" Jean-Claude threw up his hand as if to block a Waalo poisoned dart. "Dear Mambéty, I cannot bear it!"

"Still?"

"Oui...," Jean-Claude's voice trailed off. "It was not what I wanted."

"No."

"No," Jean-Claude affirmed softly.

"Good Cousin." Mambéty's voice resonated its full, commanding baritone. "Opa Pieter taught us to accept what is. None of this is what we *want*.

"Do I delight in capturing Alkebulans and sending them to such a fate as awaits them? No!

"It is necessary. I do what is necessary." Mambéty stared hard at his pale-skinned Vumbi relative, then said, "As men, we must *accept* what we cannot change.

"What happened that day was...unfortunate." After a protracted pause, Mambéty said, with a softer voice, "Did I want to carry Cheikh Anta's body back to Lebu'ta? Huh?

"Do penance if you must, but accept what is."

The men walked in strained silence that stretched several paces. Finally, Jean-Claude blurted, "You are correct," though inwardly lamented. *She is lost to me—morts. Only Jésus resurrects les morts.*

His thoughts cleared as the thick baobab trees that lined the footpath thinned. They had arrived at the end of the path near the waterfall. This was the edge of Lebu'ta.

Jean-Claude stood behind Mambéty, who said. "Wait here. I will get the boy."

"Oui." He sat on a nearby tree stump, removed a boot, and massaged his bunion. *I must focus on the* nègres *I need to settle my debts before I lose my soul in this place, as did Opa Pieter.* The Frenchman watched his Alkebulan relative grow smaller and smaller until he seemed to disappear over the horizon.

Chapter 20

Draughts

Ten pegs stood tall atop an ornate board of interlocking carved woods. Felled black and brown pegs lay strewn on either side.

Adama and Awa's casual game of draughts had become more intense. Adama was winning. But it was Awa's turn. She hesitated, then moved an ebony peg diagonally two squares towards her opponent.

Adama's eyes swept the board of alternating light and dark squares. He fingered a mahogany peg, and then a long shadow fell across the board.

The children looked up. Mambéty's green eyes stared back. The prince smiled. The princess frowned.

"Uncle Mambéty," Adama said, "you are well?"

"Pape, you are blocking the sun."

"Quiet child," Mambéty scolded Awa, "I have no interest in your game of draughts. And where are your manners? Your yaye would be ashamed of such a greeting."

"She is just mad because I am winning," Adama said, still smiling.

"Yes, yes. The game can wait. Come with me Adama."

"Where are you taking him, Father?"

"Where are we going Uncle?"

"Do not question me. Just come!"

Adama jumped up quickly. His jerky movements knocked the board. The standing pegs tumbled over and rolled—most off the table.

"Sorry," Adama said. He and Awa stooped to pick up the pieces.

"Do not go Adama," Awa whispered.

Adama looked at her quizzically and shrugged as if to ask *why not.*

"You are in danger. Run to maam bu góor," she said, still whispering.

"Leave the game boy and come," Mambéty directed.

Awa watched as Adama and her father walked away. She turned and ran to find her maam bu góor.

Chapter 21

Secret Writing

"Bonjour mon jeune ami!" Jean-Claude greeted Adama jovially.

Always excited to see the exotic-looking Vumbi, Adama returned the salutation enthusiastically.

"Bonjour Monsieur le Capitaine." The prince continued speaking in French, "It is very good to see you again."

"Yes, yes," Mambéty interrupted, "Enough of that for now. We want to know if you can read this." He produced the scroll and held it for Adama to see.

The prince took the scrolled writing from his uncle, peered at the markings, and said, "It is Arabic, I think."

Jean-Claude and Mambéty exchanged looks.

"Well, what does it say, Adama? Will the sun set before you tell us?"

"Give the boy a chance, Mambéty," Jean-Claude said calmly.

"It says, Greetings generous Kilifa Ibrahima N'Diaye, Good Spirit and wise Lamane of the great nation of Lebu'ta." Adama used his finger to trace the writing from right to left. "Allah has answered my dua if this writing finds you well.

"You are a true friend of our jihad. Continue to stand with me against the kings who feed people to the Vumbi. Those who would sell their own neighbors without care for what awaits them at the bottom of those horrible ships.

"Those who will bring ruin to our land, for we will soon have no farmers, fishermen, or artisans.

"In a fortnight from the last full moon, Sidy the Baol, my chief of war, will cross the Senegal River and invade Waalo. He requires warriors from Lebu'ta to stand ready at your northern border. Great Lamane of Lebu'ta, allow no Waalo to escape into the Baobab Forest as they flee our Marabout and Baol warriors.

"My messengers, Karenga and Ahmed, are trustworthy. Give your response to them. I await it." Adama ran his fingertip over an embossed Arabic emblem of curved lines, then said, "Nasir Al-Din, servant of Allahu Akbar."

Adama looked at his uncle and le capitaine, then back at the writing." More is here at the bottom." The prince pointed at the hastily written script.

"Friend Kilifa, descendant of the Burba N'Diadiane N'Diaye, there is treachery close to the heart of Lebu'ta. Take steps of protection, lest you suffer greater losses." Adama stopped reading. He looked quizzical at his uncle.

Mambéty snatched the writing from Adama's hand and said, "Good."

"That writing is to maam bu góor," the prince said hesitantly.

Jean-Claude locked his green eyes on Mambéty's.

"That is not your concern," Mambéty said crossly.

"But..." Adama's voice trailed off.

The Frenchman surreptitiously shook his head, then said to the prince, "Do not worry mon jeune ami. Your grandfather will get the writing, I assure you."

"Yes, yes," Mambéty chimed in, "I will discuss this with the good Lamane shortly." He guided the prince back towards Lebu'ta.

"But really, Adama, that is none of your affair. The Lamane spoils you such that you no longer know your place.

"If I find that you have spoken of this to anyone, including Awa, I will feed you to the bukki!"

Adama trembled. His first thought had been to tell Awa.

Chapter 22

Collaborator

The small, dark room smelled of urine and spoiled meat. Bits of fresh air slipped in through the spaces between the wooden slats. It did little to quell the noxious scents of the unwashed Vumbi sailors and guardsmen who occupied the makeshift ale house.

Mambéty and Jean-Claude sat at a table drinking in a curtained-off corner. Signare Alimatou peered around the cloth that hung from a rope and smiled. The pair's hushed tones fell to silence.

"Good Signare Alimatou. How wonderful to see you," Mambéty said. "I am surprised you come in such a place as this."

"Mmmm," the signare purred. "I do not often come here it is true. But when messieurs of distinction, like yourself and le capitaine de Visé do me the honor of patronage, naturally, I hurry over."

"Ah. Merci. How is business?" Jean-Claude inquired.

"This place," she said, looking at the dirty walls, "makes more than I expected. It is mostly for people who do not wish to be seen or overheard." She smiled slyly at the cousins.

"Also, the guardsmen and seamen need a place to go when their livres are low. They would make trouble otherwise. It helps preserve the peace on the island, so my merchant business can thrive. So, I keep it open.

"Might you need my services?" Signare Alimatou asked, looking at Mambéty.

"I do not involve myself in such dealings," Mambéty answered curtly. "Leave us to drink your horrible ale in peace. Send your boy with some victuals. We have been waiting too long."

"Many pardons," she said.

The signare withdrew, bowing her head slightly. The curtain fell back in place. The two men waited briefly before continuing their whispered conversation.

"I will need at least 150," Jean-Claude said.

"Aaugh! That is a tall request. I have arranged to get 50 from Garmi the Waalo, who will trade for some of the guns you brought."

"That is not enough, mon ami. There must be a nearby fishing village we can raid."

Mambéty shook his head. "I met you many seasons ago, Jean-Claude. We were both young. This is only your fourth sailing, but I *live* here and have seen the changes.

"Never have I been to your country. If I dared go to France, or any Vumbi country, could I buy people mon cousin?"

Mambéty's tone was very somber and introspective. Jean-Claude watched him closely as he spoke.

"Throughout the seasons, many ships come. Before we were born, the ships came. Even before Opa Pieter, other ships came here and took people. Different Vumbi, but really all the same. And the ships are getting bigger and harder to fill."

"Ah! There are plenty of people still," Jean-Claude interjected dismissively with a flip of his hand.

"Hmm. What is brought to trade gets smaller."

"Times are hard, Mambéty. I have many debts. I have brought the best of what I could afford."

"So you say, Jean-Claude," Mambéty retorted and swallowed some ale. "But where are we to get 100 more people?"

"The fishing village to the north of Lebu'ta seems large enough. I saw it coming into port."

"I am uncertain. Uneasy. Over the many seasons, the fishermen have been hit often. Now, they hardly fish. Those that remain mostly use their longboats for hire as transports to the ships. If we raid the fishermen, how will we get the people on the ships, Jean-Claude?"

"What about the Banju? They are mere farmers and could not repel us," replied le capitaine.

"Too many farmers have been taken already. The smart ones move further from the shore and seek alliances. No. In this, Lamane Kilifa is correct. We will soon starve."

"You will not starve, mon ami cousin," Jean-Claude said, shaking his head emphatically.

"No. When you become Lamane, you must rule with an iron fist. Yes, and make farmers out of the kings you conquer. This is why I bring you firearms. You must take control of Lebu'ta—"

Mambéty cut in, "You are generous, mon capitaine cousin! And all I must do is fill your ships. Ah!"

"Of course, cousin. That is the best use of our relationship," Jean-Claude said.

"You get rich in France, and I, ha, I run the risk of ending up in one of those boats myself one day."

"You worry too much, cousin Mambéty. Now that Adama's father is disposed of, we will both get what we want."

Mambéty glared at his relative. "You vile Vumbi! You are like a vulture who feasts on the living. You who cried when your prey was felled by a Waalo dart before you could...Ah! I will never understand you, Jean-Claude. You mistook her kindness. She would never have betrayed—"

"Come, come! It is true, I sometimes am melancholy over Cheikh Anta's wife. But I rebound, as you advised me to do, mon cousin.

"S'il vous plaît, no more recriminations. We should not quarrel. Let us put our heads together and plan wisely. I have not much time here. And the epistle puts Nasir Al-Din's chief Sidy the Baol on our heels," Jean-Claude said.

A boy brought bread and cheese on a tray with more ale. The men grunted at the interruption. The child backed out of the corner.

"We must move swiftly," Jean-Claude said. He broke off a piece of hard brown bread and devoured it.

Chapter 23

Lake Retba

Djibril slid away soon after Gorgui completed his lesson for the day. Samba and some other children noticed him go but thought little of it. Elders often filled their free time with chores or more learning.

Samba sauntered to a group of boys engaged in a game of skill. He watched them play, all the while glancing over his shoulder at two other boys a few meters away.

Prince Adama and Malick, the objects of Samba's interest, talked animatedly in hushed tones. Undoubtedly, Samba could not hear their words. He moved closer.

"I do not think we should go," Adama told Malick.

"We must go, or we will live in shame under the heels of Djibril and Samba," Malick replied.

"Awa had a bad omen and told me I should not leave Lebu'ta."

"Ah!" Malick threw up his hands. "Awa is a *girl*. Adama, we are boys and soon to be men. You want to be Lamane, do you not?"

Adama nodded.

"Well then, you must prove your merit. We will find Lake Retba and bring back some of the pink water. Show Djibril and Samba, then splash it in their faces!"

The boys giggled.

"What are you laughing at?" Samba asked Malick, whom he now stood beside.

"We are laughing at you," replied Malick, who turned to face the interloper. "We are going on an adventure to find Lake Retba."

Samba's eyes stretched wide.

"May I come too?" he asked.

Malick and Adama consulted wordlessly, then nodded. The three boys drew closer together.

Samba said, "We will need water, bread—"

"Ah! Ah! You do not tell us what to do," Malick reproached. "I am in charge. *I say* we bring water, bread...um...we will need protection from the bukki."

"I have a knife," Adama offered.

"Me too." Malick said to Samba, "You?"

"Yes."

"Good. Adama, bring your spinning needle to help us find our way."

"When do we go?" Samba asked.

"Right away. We go back pack our bags, and meet at the stone nest. Hurry!"

The three boys sprinted past Awa, who played nearby, and heard Malick say, 'meet at the stone nest.' The princess watched Adama run and shivered.

Awa bade Khadija and Yacine farewell and walked to the nearby clearing where large stones had been placed in an ancient formation by an unknown people. She had learned that the stones, which stood taller than she, were there when the Lebu'tans arrived in the land.

Shortly, Adama and Malick arrived. The pair talked excitedly, showed their knives, and admired Adama's rudimentary compass. Samba ran up behind them.

"Where are you going?" Awa asked.

The three boys jumped, then turned to see where the voice came from. Malick groaned audibly when he saw the princess who stood next to one of the stones. Her eyes fixed on the prince.

"We are going to Lake Retba to bring back some of the pink water." Adama tried to sound stoic.

"You should not leave Lebu'ta Adama. If you go beyond the sacred baobab trees, you will not come back." Awa warned.

"Do not listen to her," Samba said.

"Hush, Samba," Malick snapped, "Djibril is not here to protect you from me."

"You said that I was in danger when I went with your pape. Nothing bad happened." Adama paused, then said, "Well, nothing... um...nothing I can talk about."

"Come Adama. Let us go," Malick urged.

The boys slung their bags onto their backs and walked towards the Baobab Forest that marked the edge of Lebu'ta.

Awa followed.

As they passed the first row of trees, Adama turned and looked at Awa who still trailed them.

Malick frowned. "You cannot come with us Awa. Go back to the heart of Lebu'ta. You are a girl!"

"I know what I am Malick. I do not need you to tell me."

She continued to follow them and nothing more was said.

The four children, dwarfed by the gigantic trees of the forest, walked with what appeared to be great confidence. Scant light came through the tangled branches of the strange-looking trees. Yet, it was enough to illuminate an oft-used footpath. The crushed grass ran alongside a baobab large enough for all of them to fit inside, if hollowed out.

They walked quietly, save for the sounds of breaking twigs. Each looking upwards at some of the tallest trees in the forest. The ripe, elongated baobab fruit they often ate hung from the sturdy branches. A particularly dense cluster of branches plunged the travelers into temporary premature dusk.

Abruptly, Awa gasped. All eyes followed her slender, bejeweled finger, which pointed to an enormous baobab.

A twisted ankle and sandaled foot protruded from the base of a hollowed tree. Nearby, an Alkebulan rock python uncoiled itself and slithered into the darkness.

Chapter 24

Hollow Hallowed Tree

The noise of insects, birds, snakes, and other small creatures grew louder. Nature seemed to offer this dirge for the young man Awa found stuffed inside a sacred baobab tree trunk.

The four children gathered around the horribly repugnant discovery. Like all Lebu'tan children, they were comfortable with the circle of life, but unacquainted with what appeared to be a senseless taking of human life.

Adama looked quizzically at the small, embossed medallion fastened to the band on the dead man's ankle.

"We must get him out of there," Malick said. "It is not right. A body should be treated with dignity in death as in life."

Adama, Malick, and Samba tugged at the stiff, cold limb. The body jerked forward, banged against the inside of the trunk, then fell backwards.

Malick stopped tugging. "He's stuck."

"Maybe we can widen the opening with our knives," Adama suggested.

The boys rifled through their bags, finally producing their small weapons. In so doing, much of the contents had tumbled onto the ground.

Malick and Adama dug their blades into the massive tree trunk. Samba joined in, jabbing and poking energetically. Flecks of bark stuck to the boys' sweaty brows. Samba stopped, stood back, and wiped his face in the crook of his arm. He looked over at Awa.

"We should go back and get one of the elders," the princess advised. She clutched her cowrie shell necklace. Her tight, twisting grip frayed its cord.

Samba quietly nodded his head in agreement.

Adama and Malick kept working.

"Did you hear that?" Samba asked.

"Be quiet, Samba. You are just frightened," Malick answered.

"No! Listen," the boy insisted.

Malick and Adama stood still. "I do not hear anything, Samba."

"I heard it too," said Awa.

Samba looked this way and that. "We must go back, Malick," he said urgently.

Adama looked at Samba, then turned his head back to the protruding leg. He stared hard at the medallion's clear curved lines. He recognized the Arabic.

"Okay. But remember, it is you who are afraid, Samba. Adama and I are brave. We are almost men!"

The prince looked over at Samba triumphantly. "Yes, we are almost men," he echoed. With a less confident voice, he said, "But we should go back now."

Adama dusted off his spinning needle. Malick and he peered at the gyrating indicator. "We go that way." The prince pointed towards the direction from which they came, then slipped the compass into his pocket.

The boys packed up everything but their knives, which they held in their hands. The four children walked two by two on the path back home. No one noticed Awa's necklace fall to the ground.

Suddenly, the living creatures of the woods became silent. This rendered the otherwise quiet *crack-snap* sound quite audible. The children exchanged quick glances, then ran.

Waalo raiders emerged from the thicket. The men ran swiftly behind the children. The Waalo seemed to be everywhere at once.

A raider grabbed Samba, and the boy screamed, "Help me!" The raider's violent embrace pinned Samba's arms to his sides, rendering his weapon useless. "Help me!" he cried out again.

Malick stopped abruptly and turned back. With an outstretched arm holding his glinting knife, he rushed at the Waalo who held Samba. The blade went deep into the raider's arm, and the man released the boy with a howl.

The two children ran towards Lebu'ta. After sprinting several meters alongside Samba, Malick looked to one side, then the other. Finally he glanced over his shoulder.

"Where are Adama and Awa?" Malick yelled the question.

Samba answered him not. The boys ran faster.

Chapter 25

Royal Captives for Sale

Awa's father, Mambéty, paced impatiently. "Are you sure they are coming?" he asked in French.

His cousin, the privateer Capitaine Jean-Claude, nodded. "Oui. Très bientôt."

Frowning, Moustapha asked, "What is it that you say, Mambéty?" Clearly annoyed, Djibril's father continued, "You know I do not speak that dreadful Vumbi language!"

"It is nothing, my friend. We must wait for the Waalo," Mambéty said in the common tongue. "Jean-Claude says they will be here very soon."

The big man grunted, still annoyed. Mambéty and he, Moustapha, along with a few other Lebu'tans, Jean-Claude, and three of le capitaine's crewmen, waited on the outskirts of Lebu'ta.

The clearing, in which the band of men stood, sat, or paced, lay almost half a kilometer from the spot where the children had found the dead man in the live baobab tree.

Moustapha's head swiveled back and forth. He watched Mambéty pace whilst Jean-Claude and his crewmen tended to their firearms. Finally, the big man stood, massaged his neck, and ambled over to his fellow sons of the earth. He spoke affably with the men in the common tongue. Within moments, the forest became loudly animated. Moustapha turned towards the commotion, as did everyone else.

Like a ravenous bukki pack in a bad dream, Waalo raiders emerged from the bush, dragging their tethered prey. Moustapha's mouth dropped open at the sight of the raiders and captives.

The clearing quickly became crowded with double rows of men, women, and children bound at the neck with forked sticks. Each captive's hands were securely fastened together by a coarse rope behind their backs. There were more than 50 souls in all. Jean-Claude's eyes roamed over the bodies. He licked his lips and smiled.

A sour taste settled at the back of Moustapha's throat. He hocked and spat on the ground, then looked upon each sorrowful face.

One of the boys, his torso thick and brown, looked like Moustapha's son Djibril. Watching the child's fear-filled eyes proved too much for the big man, who turned away.

He glared at Mambéty, who had talked him into this act of treasonous treachery. If caught, the Lamane, strictly against slavery, would react harshly to their disobedience. *Could he trust that sneaky griot Gorgui? Ah! What to do.* Moustapha's reflections were interrupted.

"Let go of me!" The words were carried on a breeze past Moustapha to Mambéty.

"Awa?" Mambéty called out. He stiffened as Garmi, the leader of the Waalo raiders, came into view with his daughter and nephew in tow.

"Release her at once!" Mambéty yelled.

The princess ran to her father.

"Uncle Mambéty! Uncle Mambéty!" Adama cried. "Monsieur le Capitaine!"

"The boy too," Mambéty said somewhat reluctantly.

Garmi, the Waalo holding Adama, pushed the prince onto the ground. Freed, he scampered over to Awa.

"Eh? Are we not here to sell captives? To raid for more captives?"

growled Garmi, whose arm still bled from Malick's prick. "These two are worth much. If you want them, you must pay for them."

Moustapha observed Mambéty and Jean-Claude exchange glances. He grimaced.

When I summoned Djibril, I should have sent for the other royal children as well. Gorgui should have advised this. Wretched little man. Moustapha thought crossly.

How did they fall into the hands of the Waalo? No matter. Prince Adama and Princess Awa see all who are here. They will surely tell their maam bu góor.

The big man groaned audibly as he thought through the situation, desperately searching his mind for a palatable solution. *What to do now? Kill them both? Mambéty will not suffer me to kill his precious Awa.* "Ah!" he said.

Whilst Moustapha pondered his calamity, he seemed oblivious to the screams and sobs of the captives. Now, no longer focused inward, he found their loud clamoring distressing.

Moustapha's eyes settled on the captive who resembled Djibril. The child seemed to sense Moustapha watching him, for he returned the gaze with red, bruised, accusing eyes.

Bad omen. Moustapha's heart sank. He wrapped one meaty hand over another in succession. His dream of Djibril marrying Awa disappeared. *Djibril Lamane of Lebu'ta? Ha! How could I have been so foolish?*

Anger, fear, and self-loathing bubbled up, mixed, and curdled Moustapha's thoughts. He clenched his hands hard. The small cuts from the trek through the forest widened. Blood pooled in the slits, trickled over, under, and around, settling in the palms of his hands—hands that may soon be cut off by Lamane Kilifa.

Chapter 26

The Great Baol Horsemen

Scores of hooves kicked up considerable dirt on an earthen road. From a distance, it looked as if an endless sea of horsemen sailed on waves of tawny mist.

Sidy and his Baol warriors had just crossed the mighty Senegal River into Mauritania. They moved swiftly towards the encampment of Nasir Al-Din, leader of the Marabout Jihad.

"Great Warrior." A muscular, bare-chested horseman spoke loudly as he rode up alongside the war chief.

"Good Zenaga. Speak!" Sidy yelled to be heard over the horses' thunderous pounding and the clanging of battle armaments.

"Is it wise to join our tested brethren with these Marabouts... these Muslim devotees?"

The war chief laughed heartily, yet the wooden breastplate, strapped across his broad chest, barely moved.

"Al-Din's men are worthy. They have won many battles and will double our number," Sidy said. "All mine to command...and yours, as my second."

The great Baol war chief and Zenaga rode in silence. The encampment now clearly visible on the horizon.

"Great Warrior, it is said Al-Din fights the raiders only to spread his religion. When my talon blade flies," Zenaga said, touching one of the double-bladed weapons belted on his horse, "like a hawk, it does not look to see if the prey is Vumbi or Muslim."

"Nor mine," said the big-boned, powerfully built commander. "We free captives. All others die!"

"That is *our* wisdom. The Waalo raiders stole *our* children and wives, not Al-Din's," Zenaga said wrathfully.

Sidy looked at his trusted second and nodded. "I, too, grieve my beloved sister. She is dead. But her son? I look for his face in each child we rescue from slavers."

"The boy is lost, Great Warrior. The raiders do not keep captives in Alkebulan, where we can find them.

"No. The boy was surely taken to Gorée Island and put on a dreadful Vumbi ship." Only Zenaga would say such a thing to Sidy. The warriors had known each other since boyhood.

"I consume this knowledge, Good Zenaga, but I still drink hope," Sidy said. "The alliance will help us drive the Vumbi out before they devour us all.

"Al-Din wants us to spare as many Alkebulans as we can. Leave them to his Marabout devotees to save or slaughter."

"Unwise," Zenaga said. "We may suffer much waiting for Al-Din to learn that the Waalo and other Alkebulan nations make poor Muslims."

"Yes," Sidy agreed. "His plan is folly. Until his eyes open, we will have use of his Marabouts and convert the Vumbi to carrion!" The war chief leaned forward on his black steed, squeezed his calves on the animal's flesh, and whooped, "Woola-la-la-la-la!"

Chapter 27

Royal Captives for Sale

The midday sun shone brightly upon Sidy and his mighty warriors who rode hard at full gallop. They leaned into the wind, which blew free-flowing sweat from their brows.

All but Zenaga wore mud cloth covered wooden armor, soiled with blood and bits of bone from skirmishes with the Waalo. The Baol cloth had various clan patterns, while the Mauritanians had the Arabic symbol الله أكبر—*God is Great.*

It had been a hard long trek south from Mauritania. Zenaga had guided them back across the mighty Senegal River using a more eastward route to avoid encountering more Waalo bands.

Zenaga raised his metal spear high, signaling the men to stop. "Great Warrior," he pointed the weapon towards thick clusters of trees. "The Baobab Forest."

The war chief nodded. "Have the scouts returned?"

"No."

"How many sunrises?" Sidy asked.

"A full fist. But they are cunning and know the land."

"We wait," said the war chief who dismounted and sheathed his spear on his horse's belt.

Zenaga and all the warrior horsemen also descended from their mounts.

"They shall soon arrive. *Our* Baol brethren will not disappoint us." Zenaga stared at the path from the forest as if to will his scouts to appear. "Not like the Marabout messengers who failed their simple mission."

Sidy laughed a hearty laugh. "You are hard, Good Zenaga." The war chief rubbed his steed's glistening black back. "But correct. We spilled much time waiting on Al-Din's messengers, Karenga and Ahmed."

"Great Warrior, they are surely dead...the battle plans known."

The commander nodded but made no immediate reply. He listened to the murmurs of his men. *They are bored*, the war chief thought, *and anxious for true battle.*

"Yes, Good Zenaga. But are the plans known by the Lamane of Lebu'ta? If so, will he commit his men to the jihad and send them to the northern border?"

Zenaga surveyed the terrain. "We will soon know," he said. "For there is the back of Lebu'ta." He pointed at the waterfall that marked the edge of Lamane Kilifa Ibrahima N'Diaye's nation.

The war chief gazed in amazement at the breathtaking sight. "Truly, Lebu'ta is blessed!"

Sidy and the men tended to their horses—ensuring the wide belts were securely fastened to their horses' underbellies. From the belts hung sheathed swords, metal shields, and, for some, muskets. Every Baol warrior carried a metal spear or double-edged blade in hand while riding.

The war chief mounted his steed. "Good Zenaga, I tire of waiting. I go to Lebu'ta. Keep but a few men and come before the sun sets."

Sidy felt his horse tense before it vocalized a warning whinny. A moment later Malick and Samba crashed through the trees with Waalo raiders hot on their heels.

Before Sidy could raise the spear in his hand, Zenaga let fly his curved weapon. It moved through the air faster than a falcon, slicing the necks of all but one of the Waalo. The bodies sagged and thudded to the ground. The two terrified Lebu'tan boys, splattered with blood, stood with mouths agape. When Zenaga's weapon was back in his hand, he directed the Baol warriors to question the surviving Waalo.

"Bring those two boys here," Sidy commanded. He spoke loudly to be heard above the cries of the lone captured Waalo being interrogated.

Part Four

Tethered

"I dream of an Africa which is in peace with itself."

—Nelson Mandela

Chapter 28

Baol Warrior-Scouts

Anchored firmly by enormous dimensions and weight, a baobab tree stood sentry over Adama and Awa. The two children sat on the millennium-old tree's giant roots that grew high above the ground.

The makeshift slave camp in which they were remanded was fairly quiet. Mambéty, Jean-Claude, and the others had gone on a slave-raiding expedition led by Garmi. Only one Waalo raider remained in the camp. He guarded the tethered captives and watched Adama and Awa, who spoke together in low tones.

"I told you not to leave Lebu'ta," the princess whispered.

"But we are alright, Awa. Uncle Mambéty rescued us," Adama said. "Your vision should have shown you that," he added crossly.

Awa shook her head. "No. No. That is untrue," she replied. "You are such a child, Adama," the princess said in her best grown-up voice. "You know my father is Waalo, yet they demanded payment for us just like those people over there." She gestured towards the tethered men, women, and children on the other side of the camp.

"They will be taken across the water and never seen again," Awa said. "This is a terrible thing. Do you not listen when maam bu góor talks?"

The prince lowered his eyes. "Well, I did hear him tell Uncle Mambéty that the ships are horrible. But Uncle says we must do this to crush our enemies."

"Who are our enemies, Adama? Who? Those people over there? What if *we* were over there? Who would—"

The guard approached the children. His face a mask of hostility. In the Waalo tongue, the guard yelled, "Silence!"

Adama and Awa jumped. The pair looked up at the Waalo guard but said nothing for a moment. Then, the prince spoke in the watchman's own tongue.

"Good friend, we are only praying," Adama said contritely.

The guard grunted and walked a few paces away.

Turning to Awa, Adama said, "He wants us to stop talking."

"I heard him. I know Waalo, too, remember? Why did you tell him that lie?"

"I figured he would let us keep talking if he thinks we are praying."

"You should not taint sacred customs with untruths, cousin."

Awa always called Adama cousin when she was vexed with him. The princess looked across the camp at the captives and shook her head.

"We must leave this place...get back home," Awa said, barely moving her lips.

The prince shook his head. "Uncle Mambéty said we should wait here. He said we could get captured by other raiders."

"Yes, it is dangerous in the forest, but perhaps we should try just the same. If we do not, I fear you will not return to Lebu'ta."

"I do not know why you say such things, Awa. Besides, I know not where we are or how to get home."

"What about your spinning needle. Will that not show us the way to Lebu'ta?"

Adama shrugged. "We may become lost in the forest."

"Let us...try."

A little girl in great distress caught Awa's eye. Tears streamed down the girl's her fat cheeks. She struggled and squirmed, but the ropes held her fast.

The princess tore her eyes away and said to Adama, "But first, you should free that girl—and those people." Awa gestured at the captives across the camp.

Adama looked at Awa with wide eyes and an open mouth.

"Yes! There is only the one guard. Do you still have your knife?"

The prince nodded.

The princess smiled at him. "Good. I will try to distract him whilst you cut the ropes. Then we will find our way back to Lebu'ta. You must be quick!"

Before Adama could protest, Awa had stood and approached the guard. Her solemnity was outwardly apparent in her face and demeanor.

Loud guttural Waalo commands erupted from the lone watchman. "Go back, girl. You keep praying. Yes, pray Garmi sells you to Mambéty. As for me? I would sell you to the Vumbi with them!" He pointed to the more than four dozen captives on the other side of the camp.

Awa bowed her head submissively, but the tall guard continued to speak harshly. With no outward emotion, she slipped the diamond ring off her finger.

The princess' royal gemstone rocked in the open palm of her small hand. Its magnificent beauty mesmerized the guard. He gestured as if to take it, but his arm dropped to his side. The diamond's cold, colorless fire seemed to lick the finely chiseled edges of the setting.

Awa intermittently uttered low tones with throaty clicks—just as her yaye had taught her. The guard flinched but did not look away. When his heavy eyelids dropped, she fell silent.

Adama watched his betrothed. He did not move until the Waalo guard's eyes closed. Then he fished out the knife he had hidden in his clothing. The prince looked at the glinting blade. A flash of movement reflected on it. Adama raised his eyes just as the yelling began.

Several heavily weaponed Baol warriors rushed into the clearing. Three of Sidy's scouts were joined by two other warriors—and Zenaga himself. Their swords, spears, and curved double-edged talon blades slashed the air. They searched for adversaries but found only one.

Adama's mouth dropped open again as he instinctively moved away from danger. His back pressed against the rough baobab bark. Awa hurriedly rejoined her cousin at the tree. The two held hands.

Zenaga wielded a talon blade in each hand. He alone did not wear the Baol wooden armor. Like a leadwood tree, his exposed, dense torso rippled with moving muscles.

"Woorah!" Zenaga shouted the Baol war cry.

The bellow roused the lone Waalo guard who had been in a hypnotic stupor. The Baol's talon blade burrowed a deep gash in the watchman's neck. The Waalo collapsed without uttering a sound. Zenaga looked this way and that for another opponent. Spying none, he hastened to help cut the captive's ropes.

"Who are they, Adama?" the princess asked over the loud cries and tumult. The pair still held hands with their backs against the baobab tree.

"It sounds like the Baol tongue," Adama answered.

The prince recalled the writing he had translated for his uncle and le capitaine. "Maybe Al-Din's war chief...Sidy?"

Chapter 29

The Talon Blades

ambéty, Jean-Claude, Garmi, and the other raiders emerged from the forest. In tow were seventy souls bound by heavy ropes.

Adama surreptitiously hid his knife.

Mambéty and his fellow raiders quickly assessed the situation. He unsheathed his dagger, Jean-Claude unholstered his flintlock pistol, and Garmi pulled a handful of darts from his quiver. The other raiders similarly prepared to fight.

The Baol warrior-scouts turned their bladed weapons from the ropes to the necks of the Waalo, Lebu'tans and Vumbi, who had not yet fully armed themselves. The scent of blood filled the air.

Above the shouts and yowls, Jean-Claude's voice could be heard yelling oaths in French. He saw his captives, whose tethers had been cut by the Baol, escape into the forest. "No!" he bellowed.

Zenaga, the bare-chested Baol turned and sighted the Vumbi capitaine. He advanced, rotating two curved talon blades with magnificent skill and dexterity.

A thin wooden projectile flew at him—*poisoned darts*. The Baol knew that the Waalo aimed at the head to kill and the ankle to stun. He deftly deflected the dart and cut it into a sliver.

The whizzing and buzzing grew louder and more constant. The Baol instantly became a blur of seemingly random movements—forward, sideways, backward—turning around and around. Like a dancing, bladed tornado, he slashed in the direction of his turns, all the while closing in on the Vumbi and avoiding the barrage of darts.

The Baol pivoted and threw one of his talon blades at two of the raiders. The glinting curved weapon spun out fast. It seemed to chase its own handle in a deceptively fast rotation. The razor's edge sliced the neck of one of the dart-blowing Waalo. It continued to spin, with a more upward angle, and shaved off the lips of the other, before gliding back into the hand of its master like a trained hawk.

Jean-Claude's head followed the path of the talon blade. His eyes stretched wide in horror.

"Woorah!" Zenaga howled and stepped towards Jean-Claude. This movement jolted le capitaine to action. Quickly, he readied his pistol, took aim, and squeezed the trigger.

The mighty Zenaga fell backwards. The supine Baol held fast to one talon blade. The other lay beside his now dead body.

A freed captive heard the bare-chested Baol's final battle cry and recognized him as the one who had set him free. The young man looked from the talon blade, that lay beside the dead warrior-scout, to the Vumbi capitaine. Jean-Claude and the young man locked eyes, then simultaneously sprinted towards the weapon.

Le capitaine might have been as fast as his former captive but for the weight of his bulky Vumbi clothing. Jean-Claude realized midway that he would not be victorious in the race. As quickly as he could, he brought up his firearm and pulled the trigger, the muzzle still angled downward. The shot, released prematurely, lodged in his opponent's calf.

The former captive felt the slug enter his leg. The searing pain was tremendous, causing him to arch his back in mid-stride. Despite the wound, he kept running. He had never seen anything like the curved double-edged bloodied blade. It lay just two paces away and seemed more like a prize than a weapon.

Jean-Claude did not know his adversary, who had been stolen from a farm in Banju, had little knowledge of weaponry. The former captive, who had not long been initiated into manhood, would nevertheless have hewed him down, but for the Waalo poisoned dart. It pierced his skin at the neck, and he collapsed. The young farmer lay prostrate alongside his Baol liberator—his hand but a thumbnail away from the bloodied weapon.

Several other young men, cut free by the warrior-scouts, fought alongside their Baol liberators. Few had weapons, none were warriors, but all were fierce. Adama and Awa stood in the shadow of the great baobab, watching the melee.

The seventy newly captured persons, bound one to another by ropes, awkwardly fled into the forest. They moved like a crazed centipede.

"Look," Awa said, pointing. They are running away. "Why do the others not run, too?"

"Because of how they are tied," the prince responded, "they cannot run."

"Loose them, Adama. Where is your—"

Crack! The nearby report of Jean-Claude's firearm muffled the princess' words. Adama's eyes were wide with fear and amazement. The first group of captives was less than three meters from where he and Awa stood. He did not move.

"Loose them, Adama!" The princess nudged him forward.

Adama jumped down from atop the gigantic baobab root and looked up at his cousin. With sagging shoulders, Adama inched away from his perceived sanctuary.

"Hurry up!" she urged.

To the right of where he stood, Adama observed Uncle Mambéty and Djibril's father, Moustapha, fighting against the Baol warrior-scouts. Near them, Garmi blew poisoned darts in between kicks and punches.

Adama circled around and tripped over an overgrown root. He picked himself up and cast a furtive glance back. Awa dropped her face into her hands and shook her head.

The prince scrambled to his feet and scurried over to the captives. The group erupted in shouts and pleas. Adama filtered through the several languages and dialects. Most of what he could translate were appeals for help and mercy. One voice had particularly menacing undertones, but he could not decipher enough words to extract any meaning.

Adama grabbed one of the ropes that bound several people collectively. It was taut against a dark brown arm that had been rubbed raw. He sawed away at the fibers with sweaty hands. The ropes frayed and popped. The captives moved so fast to get away that it seemed they began running from a seated position.

Adama wiped his hands and continued his task. Moving down the line, the prince came to the man who continued to utter menacing-sounding words. Adama hesitated. Unlike the other captives, the man was bound singly. The captive shouted, bared sharpened teeth, in sinister tones.

Just then, a dead body dropped close to Adama's foot. A Waalo poisoned dart protruded from the unseeing eye and blood bubbled from a hole in the Baol's silenced throat. The prince recoiled. He threw a frightened look at the tethered angry man and scampered back over to Awa.

Chapter 30

Flintlock Muzzle

Blood and urine from the many felled bodies saturated the ground and permeated the air. Yet, the deadly skirmish continued with some freed captives fighting alongside the remaining Baol warrior-scouts.

The weaponless former captives successfully dislodged blow-pipes and forced several Waalo raiders to the ground. The Waalo had little advantage without their darts and fared poorly in hand-to-hand fighting.

The remaining Baol crossed swords with Vumbi crewmen amidst a thinning barrage of poison darts. In a somewhat successful flank, Moustapha and the other Lebu'tans wielded their traditional weapons—some broken and splintered.

Jean-Claude, who had the only firearm, volleyed steel balls with poor accuracy. He aimed at the Baol who were fighting Moustapha.

Crack! The shot went wide, past Mambéty, nicking a warrior-scout on the head before flying into the brush.

Jean-Claude shouted an oath in frustration. He looked back at Mambéty, who, weaponless, fought a warrior-scout hand-to-hand.

Mambéty, far from having a small frame, was nevertheless dwarfed by his opponent.

The Baol's closed hand drove a quick upward thrust to Mambéty's ribs. Mambéty doubled over, and the warrior-scout grabbed Mambéty's throat and squeezed hard. Mambéty's hands, slick with blood and sweat, clawed at the Baol's hands but could not gain purchase. Mambéty gasped and gagged until his breath stopped.

"Mon Dieu!" Jean-Claude exclaimed as he raised his flintlock pistol. The weapon held only two remaining shots. *Crack!* The shot went awry. *Crack!* The round metal projectile cut through the air. Within seconds, it found its mark and ground a hole through the exposed side of the Baol. The warrior-scout howled and clasped both hands over the wound.

Mambéty wrestled free and hastily bent to pick up the dagger lost during the struggle. The wounded Baol recovered his balance and lifted his knee towards Mambéty's face. Before the blow struck, Jean-Claude jumped and swung his heavy flintlock pistol. The butt crashed down on the Baol's head. The *crack*, as loud as his shots, foretold the death of the warrior-scout who staggered and fell to the ground. Mambéty pounced and drove his dagger deep into the Baol's neck.

Le capitaine quickly emptied black powder into the muzzle. He clamped the flask with the sulfur, charcoal, and saltpeter mix under his arm, swiftly drawing out his ramrod, inserted it, and pushed the lead round up against the black powder. But before he could jam the projectile with the ramrod, a Baol warrior-scout slammed into him.

Jean-Claude fell. The huge Baol lay on top of him. The Vumbi capitaine squirmed underneath the dead weight. A poisoned Waalo dart protruded from the warrior-scout's neck.

Suddenly, the pressure from the Baol's weight diminished. Briefly, the body hung in midair, then flew to the side. Jean-Claude looked up into Mambéty's face. Their green eyes merged, and the Vumbi smiled.

"Get up. cousin!" Mambéty said. "We have killed Nasir Al-Din's men. Those were but a small group of Baol warrior-scouts. Sidy, Al-Din's war chief, cannot be far behind."

"This is not good, cousin. Many captives have escaped. With haste, we must round them up, or all is lost," Jean-Claude said.

Mambéty nodded. "Yes. Maybe even our lives!"

Chapter 31

Recapture

An invisible line divided the makeshift slave camp between the living and the dead.

On the north side, bodies of felled Alkebulans and Vumbi men lay shoulder to shoulder. On the east side, men, women, and children stood tethered with rope and misery. In the clearing between the two, Waalo raiders collected poisoned darts from the ground.

Many of the captives, freed by the Baol warrior-scouts, had become lost in the unfamiliar Baobab Forest. They had been quickly recaptured by the Waalo raiders. Other newly stolen Alkebulans brought the count to 90 souls to be marched to the sea.

Garmi, the leader of the Waalo raiders, carefully checked the ropes that bound each neck, arm, or torso. Satisfied, he reported the numbers to Mambéty and Jean-Claude.

Le capitaine turned to Mambéty and said in a low voice, "Ahh! Only ninety. I still need sixty more. I must have at least 150 slaves!"

Mambéty made calming gestures with his hands.

Things had gone badly. This was supposed to be a quick and easy raid. Mambéty had not intended to inform the Lamane about his business with Jean-Claude, but now he must. One of the Lebu'tans in his party had been killed. The death could not be ignored, especially since Moustapha was on hand. Mambéty dared not let Moustapha have anything to hold over him. The dead man's family would have to be provided for.

The thought bounced around in Mambéty's head. *The man's family would have to be provided for.* Mambéty wheeled around abruptly. His head turned this way and that way. His eyes glided over the dead men on the north side of the camp to the gigantic baobab tree where his daughter and nephew had been sitting.

"Awa!" He bellowed, "Awa!"

The princess did not respond. Neither Awa nor Adama was anywhere to be found.

Chapter 32

Bamba the Banju

The man who had spirited the prince and princess away yelled at them continually. The more Adama tried to communicate with the former Waalo captive, the more agitated the man became.

"His teeth are like a shark's. Why is he so angry?" Adama asked Awa.

The princess gave a subtle shrug and said, "Maybe because you did not cut his ropes when you had the chance."

"He was yelling at me then, too! Probably could have gnawed through the ropes with those teeth. I think he is possessed of bad spirits. What does he want with us?"

"I do not know," Awa said, "but he has not tied us up."

"Only because he has no rope," the prince retorted. "Perhaps he will sell us and send us on the Vumbi ships. Maam bu góor says such ships are too vile to speak of. I am frightened!" Tears streamed down the prince's face, and he sobbed uncontrollably.

"No, no, Adama. We must not show fear." The young princess thumbed the tears from his face as a yaye would do. "Calm down and find out his name. You can do it."

Adama sniffled and wiped snot from his lip. He asked, *What is your name* in several Wolof and Serer dialects with no luck. The ill-tempered man growled at the prince.

Awa stood up very slowly and approached their captor genially. He returned her smile with a sneer. She utter throaty clicks and melodic tones. Her voice, gentle and subdued, wafted through the air. The man's face softened. Awa dropped to her knees and crouched forward, placing her face on downturned palms.

The man watched and exclaimed, "Alhamdulillah!"

Adama recognized the Islamic phrase and quickly asked his name.

"I am called Bamba," the man replied in Arabic.

Adama grinned so widely every tooth in his mouth was visible.

Turning to Awa, the prince said, "His name is Bamba, and he is Banju."

The princess sat up from her prostrate pose. Bamba roared a stream of angry-sounding words and shook his fist in the air. The prince recoiled.

"I do not think he knows much Arabic," Adama told his cousin.

"The Banju are Muslim, but that does not mean they know more Arabic than is in their Qur'an," she responded.

Adama chanced another question in Arabic. Much to his surprise, the man responded in quiet tones. The prince and the Banju engaged in a lively conversation.

"What is he saying Adama?"

"Slavers raided his village," the prince said. "His wife or sister, I am not sure which, was killed. Or maybe it was his crops that were trampled."

"Perhaps, dear cousin, it is not Bamba's Arabic that is bad, but yours," Awa said.

"He is not easy to understand. I am doing the best I can."

"Focus on him and not his words. Use all of your eyes Adama." Awa pointed to her own eyes, then her head, and then her heart. "Try to see who he is and not how he makes you feel."

All the while, the Banju continued talking.

Adama looked hard at the Banju and listened. After a few moments, the prince nodded. A wide grin spread across his face, then flattened.

"He thinks we are godless and have not been properly raised," Adama reported. "It seems *we* are compensation for his losses. He says he is bringing us back to Banju to work his land!"

Chapter 33

Garmi the Tracker

Mambéty knew Garmi, who possessed unparalleled skill as a slave raider, was also an exceptional tracker. He needed a tracker—a good tracker. He needed Garmi.

He looked at the Waalo with equal measures of respect, contempt, and fear. *I cannot be indebted to him.* Mambéty thought, then said, "Garmi, you demanded payment for my daughter and nephew. Where are they?"

"I know not where they are," Garmi answered, then yelled inquiries to his raiders. A few responded back.

After a brief pause, Garmi turned to Mambéty and said, "One of my men reports the Banju captive broke free and took your daughter and nephew with him into the forest."

"Which captive? Why would he take them?" Mambéty asked.

"Revenge," Garmi answered flatly.

"Revenge? What is he avenging? The raid?"

"*We* did not raid his village. That was not us. We captured him whilst he looked for his family."

"Give me understanding, Garmi," Mambéty said impatiently.

The Waalo stepped towards Mambéty. In a lower tone, he said, "The Banju is the one from Lake Retba. I recognized him, and I stand in belief that he recognized us."

Mambéty's face darkened with incredulity. But he said nothing.

"I was going to give him to you as a gift—send him far from Lebu'ta on the Vumbi ship." The Waalo watched Mambéty carefully.

"Do not play me for a fool. You give nothing."

"I will give you this, Mambéty, if the boy is as good with language as you say, the Banju will surely tell him *you* killed his pape and what became of his yaye." Garmi's response flew quicker than a poisoned dart.

Mambéty felt the words sting. He fingered his sheathed dagger and considered Garmi with whom he shared Waalo heritage. But the green eyes Mambéty inherited from his Dutch grandfather reminded everyone he encountered that he had Vumbi in his blood. More than that, he lived and loved in Lebu'ta. If this Banju spoke of Lake Retba to his daughter or nephew, he could lose everything.

"This is bad business, Garmi. Very bad business. You must get them back. All three, if you are to be paid!" Mambéty added, "Plus, we need to replace the captives we did not recapture."

"This is not part of our agreement, Mambéty. What Lebu'tan trick is this?"

"Trick?" Mambéty shouted.

"Yes, trick," Garmi shouted back. "We return to an ambush of Baol warrior-scouts and have lost nine men in battle. Fighting was not part of the agreement. Recapture of delivered captives was not part of the agreement."

"The *agreement*, Garmi, is to deliver the captives to the ship! That is where you will receive your payment of firearms." Mambéty was careful not to overplay his hand. The Waalo poisoned darts flew faster than a blink.

"This was only to be a meeting place, not a delivery," Mambéty continued. In a softer tone, he said, "Garmi, you are the best tracker in the land. Please find my daughter and nephew...before harm comes to them."

Garmi consented with a sharp nod and then said, "You are now in my quiver, Mambéty." He turned to his men, gave instructions, and departed with six raiders.

Chapter 34

Pape's Name

A flock of seagulls flew overhead. Their unified cry, so loud and mournful, Adama, Awa, and even Bamba turned their heads skyward. But Awa quickly looked away, covered her ears, and moaned.

Adama and Bamba, who had been picking fruit, stared at Awa briefly then continued their work. They dropped the edibles on the grassy ground and sat down beside her.

The Banju spoke to Adama in Arabic. In response, the prince turned to the princess and asked, "What is it Awa?"

She looked at her cousin and said, "Ask Bamba if he has ever seen Lake Retba."

"Lake Retba? That is not important now. It was Malick's idea to go to Lake Retba. He is not here." Low and reflective, Adama said, "He and Samba got away."

Awa appeared not to be listening. "Ask Bamba if he has ever seen Lake Retba," she repeated.

"As you wish," he sighed. The prince turned and spoke to Bamba. The Banju drew back his lips, exposing sharp teeth. He spoke in

120

a rush, saying much more than Adama could interpret—until he uttered the name Mambéty.

"Mambéty?" Adama repeated, "Awa's pape? Do you know him?"

Awa did not wait for the Banju to answer. Knowingly she asked, "When did you see my pape at Lake Retba?" She spoke in Waalo, the native language of her pape—the tongue Adama had not tried in his attempts to communicate with the Banju.

Bamba stared hard at the princess. He ran his tongue over his sharp teeth, and in clear, precise Waalo, he said, "When he killed Lebu'ta!"

Awa returned his stare, then lowered her gaze to a grassless patch of earth near her crossed legs. Her eyes, wet with tears, squeezed closed.

Adama's mouth dropped open, and his body went rigid.

Bamba the Banju tore into a baobab fruit, untroubled by the reactions of the prince and princess.

Chapter 35

Baobab Tree

Adama and Awa sat with their backs hunched as if they each carried a heavy weight. Neither the prince nor the princess had uttered a word since Bamba the Banju declared Mambéty had killed Lebu'ta.

"I see you do not know this," Bamba told Adama in the Waalo tongue. "But she knows," he pointed at Awa.

The princess shook her head. "I do not know—*not truly.*"

Bamba took a huge bite of fruit, swallowed, and then said, "You were not there to see, so you could not know from your eyes. But you have knowledge *beyond* what your eyes see. Is this not true?" Baobab fruit dripped from his chin onto the ground.

"That is why the birds from the sea distress you so much. They carry home the sorrow of the stolen souls chained in the bellies of the Vumbi ships. Is this not true?"

Awa did not respond.

"Garmi hunts the fishermen, farmers, and villagers. They steal our people...maybe my son. He and his raiders shame the Waalo name and kill our future. Garmi hunts, and Mambéty sells to the Vumbi. Mambéty wanted Cheikh Anta's help to convince the

Lamane. When he refused, Mambéty killed Cheikh Anta—he killed Lebu'ta."

Suddenly, Adama shouted, "I do not believe you! Uncle Mambéty did not kill my pape. Why do you speak what is not true... not possible...I do not believe you!"

"Have respect and know your place, boy! I was there." Bamba thumped his chest. Bits of sticky pulp marked the spot. "Yes, I was there." He prolonged the 'I' importantly.

"How did you come to be there, Good Bamba?" Awa asked.

"My son—may Allah protect him—took sick. His yaye could not heal him. The hands of the elders did not restore him. We thought he would surely die! They sent me to fetch healing pink water from the lake.

"I ran and walked and ran—with my mind only on my son. When I entered the Baobab Forest, tired and hungered, I looked for a tree with the best fruit and the strongest branches. Allah is merciful! I found one that dripped juice from ripeness and stood thick and tall. I climbed to the top, ate, rested, and ate some more.

"When my belly smiled with fullness, my mind returned to my son. Before I climbed down, I looked about to see which way I should go. Over this way," Bamba gestured with his hand, "a daughter of Lebu'ta ran into the forest. Near the waterfall, royal guards pursued her! Worse, there was a Vumbi—the same Vumbi from today—near the clearing. I wanted to yell a warning, but I was no longer alone.

"I saw great Prince Cheikh Anta, his own royal traveling guards, and Mambéty the Waalo, who lives as a Lebu'tan, walking on the path near my tree. The great Prince and Mambéty spoke Waalo with loud voices. Cheikh Anta's traveling guards could not have understood the Waalo tongue, or else they would have foreseen danger.

"Mambéty fingered his dagger, and I knew Shaytan had whispered wickedness into his ear," Bamba said. "Just then, I saw movement. It was that vile slave raider, Garmi, hiding with his men off in the brush—a trap!

"Just as Mambéty and Cheikh Anta's words became blows, the

daughter of Lebu'ta screamed. She must have moved as fast as a leopard, as I had not seen her get so close. Yet there she was, fighting the Vumbi's evil embrace. May Allah have mercy upon her!

"Cheikh Anta turned, and Mambéty attacked him from behind. Before the royal traveling guards could intervene, Garmi's darts flew high and pierced their necks. They fell...dead.

"The daughter of Lebu'ta, still in the clutches of the Vumbi, cried out again to the great Prince. Her voice seemed to inflame Cheikh Anta, who lifted Mambéty up and dashed him onto a sharp rock. He ran towards her and surely would have killed the Vumbi had Mambéty not arisen and struck him in the back with that dagger he wears still.

"Seeing this, the daughter of Lebu'ta became wild. Then I heard Garmi's dart fly, and I saw her body lose life.

"I turned from the pitiable sight. Garmi must have seen my movement in the tree, for darts flew up at me! Allah had mercy on me—none pierced my skin. Mambéty put his dagger in its home, picked up one of the fallen darts, and pushed the tip into the great Prince's neck.

"The other guards who pursued the daughter of Lebu'ta had entered the forest. They were too late, too loud, and too blinded by the trees. Hearing their footsteps and shouts, Garmi and the Vumbi tarried no more. They lifted the body and carried the daughter of Lebu'ta away, leaving no trace.

"Mambéty held Cheikh Anta in his arms. I could see his face wet with tears. But he could not undo his treachery. He had killed Lebu'ta!"

"No!" wailed Adama.

"Yes. I tell you, yes! Mambéty used the same Vumbi dagger fighting the Baol warriors—it is not one easily forgotten. When he sells you, Lamane Kilifa's blood will end—Lebu'ta is already dead, for I am sure the Lamane knows what Mambéty has done."

"No!" Adama shouted again. Tears streamed down his face.

Awa sighed heavily. She, too, was crying.

"I tell you yes!" Angrily, Bamba shifted his small eyes from Adama to Awa, then said, "The girl knows it. She has seen it in spirit but is afraid of what she sees. And Cheikh Anta's book—the luminosity Lebu'ta is so proud of—she knows Mambéty has it but says nothing. Yes, Lebu'ta is dead because it has too much fear to live!"

Bamba's hazel eyes glinted with flecks of brown and green. He grinned, ran his tongue over his teeth, and said, "I am your light-bearer! I have restored your life with truth. Get up, you will come with me to—" Bamba's words were cut short as Garmi and his Waalo raiders sprang into view.

Chapter 36

Find the Prince & Princess

Kilifa, the Great Lamane of Lebu'ta, felt old. He paced, as was his custom when he was upset. He stopped and looked upon the ancient stone wall. His thoughts, as numerous as its glyph carvings, danced with deep dread.

The miracle that dropped Malick and Samba into the midst of the Baol horsemen was no consolation. Kilifa was indeed grateful to Sidy for the safe return of the boys. But what of his beloved Adama and Awa? And what of Moustapha's son Djibril? That was the question that most vexed the Lamane.

Why was Djibril not with the other four children? Coincidence? Perhaps. Or had Moustapha known of the Waalo slave raid? Ah! Most certainly Mambéty and that Vumbi, Jean-Claude, are involved in this treachery. But Mambéty would not allow any harm to befall his own daughter. Surely if Awa is safe, so is Adama.

Could the children be found? Should he divert Sidy to look for them? Was his single grieving heart greater than the multitude of souls Sidy could save by invading Waalo, then the Sine Kingdom as planned?

The Lamane groaned audibly. He needed time to grapple with his selfish desires. But it seemed time had been abducted too. Kilifa straightened his back and lifted his head regally as his armor-bearer approached.

"Good spirit of Lebu'ta, Great Lamane of the land. I pray for your long life," the armor-bearer said on bended knee. "I have received news of the death of scouts sent by Nasir Al-Din's Chief of War, Sidy. Their bodies were found in the Baobab Forest. This was also found." He held a cowrie shell necklace with glyph markings. "It has been identified as Princess Awa's," the armor-bearer said.

Kilifa took the necklace. He remained silent. He knew the armor-bearer had more to report.

"We also have received word that Banju has been raided again. Few were spared and the crops will surely rot."

"Banju is the basket that feeds many. There will be famine in the land." At that moment, Kilifa knew he would not delay Al-Din's plan. "Where is the war chief?" he asked.

"He and his men are in the belly of Lebu'ta taking nourishment. Shall I take you to him?"

Kilifa nodded. His armor-bearer rose. Neither observed that the griot Gorgui stood in the corner of the room, his back pressed against the wall.

"Send a fist of my guards to search for Adama and Awa," Kilifa said. "When...*if* Mambéty and Moustapha return, bring them to me!"

"I will see to it," the armor-bearer replied.

The two men walked silently towards where Sidy and his men refreshed themselves. Gorgui withdrew and departed.

A few meters along the footpath, Kilifa and his armor-bearer could hear loud voices. It was impossible to tell if the raucous was Baol's merriment or ire. Kilifa made a silent prayer. His Lebu'tan warriors, though well trained, would not suffer any disrespect from Baol.

Kilifa hastened his steps and lengthened his strides. When he and his armor-bearer came to the end of the footpath, they stood still and silent. Neither would betray their outward appearance of calm and poise by speaking before their arrival was proclaimed.

The animal skins pulled taut over a wood shell thumped loudly. All heads turned towards Lamane Kilifa as the talking drums announced his arrival.

Part Five

Île of Horror

"Darkness cannot drive out darkness, only light can do that."

—Dr. Martin Luther King, Jr.

Chapter 37

Found Again

Adama, Awa and Bamba the Banju were escorted back to the raiders' encampment with little fanfare. The children dragged their feet and were prodded roughly by the Waalo warriors. The trek back to the encampment was quick and quiet, save for the cracking twigs underfoot.

Mambéty stood near a felled tree practicing throws with his dagger. He turned and saw the group emerge from the forest wall and enter the clearing. He sheathed the stone hilt dagger and smiled.

"Awa!" he breathed her name as he rushed over to the princess. She stood motionless, frowning deeply. He picked her up and hoisted her small body high above his head then clasped her to his massive chest.

Adama stood off to the side looking at his dusty feet.

Speaking to Jean-Claude, Mambéty said, "You have no idea how relieved I am. I thought that the Banju...well, no matter." He sighed.

Still cuddling his daughter, he bounced her lightly, as he did when she was a baby. "I am even glad that my nephew is safely in hand," Mambéty said. He ran his rough hand over Adama's bowed head. Preoccupied with his thoughts, Mambéty did not observe the countenance of the children. Neither child had uttered one word. He put Awa down. When her small feet touched the ground, she scurried over to Adama.

The children's eyes met. Awa gently took Adama's hand. She led him over to the baobab tree root that previously served as their bench. With somber faces, they sat quietly. They resembled an old married couple facing grave news together.

Djibril's father, Moustapha, eyed the sullen children. Moustapha did not dislike Adama. He just felt his son Djibril would make a better Lamane. Lebu'ta needed strong leadership, and he doubted if Adama would grow into the excellence that was Cheikh Anta.

Moustapha put down the rock he was using to sharpen his knife. *Why did I let Mambéty talk me into this foolishness?* He regretted joining Mambéty on this slave raid. Everything that could go wrong had gone wrong. In retrospect it was a foolhardy endeavor. Lamane Kilifa, his uncle, would have to be told and the one person in all the land he feared was his uncle. The big man shook his head and grimaced. He ambled over to the children who sat on the overgrown root of a baobab tree.

"Adama, Awa, are you well?" Moustapha's rich baritone voice brought fresh tears to the children's eyes. "Are you hurt? Did that Banju hurt you?"

They shook their heads. More tears fell.

"Garmi the Waalo? Did he hurt you? Tell me quickly!"

"No. No one hurt us," Adama murmured weakly.

"You are unharmed. Good. Why are you crying? Where is your strength, Adama?"

"Bamba the Banju said Uncle Mambéty killed my pape. Good Bamba said he saw him do it!"

It was as if a Waalo poised dart had struck Moustapha in the heart. Cheikh Anta was Moustapha's cousin. From childhood, the two fought constantly. Nevertheless, they would protect each other if ever a third party became involved. A strained, antagonistic relationship that always seemed on the verge of collapse, Moustapha felt deep sorrow and pain at the death of Good Cousin Cheikh Anta.

Mambéty had said he and Cheikh Anta were attacked by Waalo assassins on their way back from the big meeting. That he, Mambéty, had fought off the attackers, but too late to save Cheikh Anta. At the time Moustapha was suspicious and doubted the probity of the story. His cousin, whom he fought often enough, was an excellent fighter, and the Waalo were known for poisoned darts, not knives. Ultimately, Mambéty convinced Moustapha that Cheikh Anta's death was meant to happen. The ancestors desired Moustapha's son, Djibril, to marry Awa and one day become Lebu'ta's Lamane.

"I want to go home Good Cousin Moustapha. Please, take me home to maam bu góor," Adama cried.

"Take me too," Awa chimed in.

"Shh, shh, shh! Children. Be quiet and stay put. You are not hurt! Stop that crying and hold your knowledge a secret, for now." Moustapha's command, uttered in his low, deep voice, quickly ceased their tears.

Chapter 38

Moustapha

Wails and moans wafted through the air. The prisoners, flanked by Waalo, were tightly tethered. The multicolored group moved along the well-used trail towards the sea.

Many of the captives were children. Some sobbed, some shrieked and others urinated as they walked. A few adults threw kicks and curses at anyone who came close enough—they received harsh blows in return.

Garmi and his Waalo raiders were undoubtedly in charge. Despite the presence of Mambéty's contingency, it was the Waalo who dispatch punishment for defiance.

Mambéty, Jean-Claude and Moustapha walked ahead of the group. The three men, talking in hushed tones, moved quickly. Their long strides, made in unison, soon put them a sizable distance from the rest.

Moustapha stopped abruptly. He stood stiffly with his hands on his waist and his elbows bowed outward. Mambéty and Jean-Claude had taken a few steps without him before they realized what happened and doubled back.

Loud voices struck the air. Mambéty placed his hand on Moustapha shoulder and spoke softly. Draping his arm around the big man's shoulder, Mambéty turned Moustapha round. The three walked together again at an unhurried pace.

Chapter 39

Betrayed

Adama and Awa stayed close to Moustapha. Randomly, the children stole looks at Bamba the Banju.

"Good Cousin Moustapha," Adama whispered. "I am tired, how much further."

"Quiet Adama!' Moustapha growled.

The young prince flinched.

"We are almost there," Awa soothed. "Breathe, Adama. Do you smell the sea?"

The prince took a deep breath and nodded. The heavy, brackish air filled his small nostrils.

The seashore crashed into view like a tsunami. Several empty longboats, held by human anchors, bounced about.

Awa snatched Adama's hand from where it dangled by his side. Quickly, the princess snapped her cowrie shell bracelet onto his wrist. The two fell out of step with the group. She whispered, "You must not be afraid, Adama. Pangool and Takhar will protect you. So will our new friend Good Bamba."

"Why do you say these things Awa? I am not going with Bamba.

He is going across the water with the other captives. You know this!" His voice was too loud.

"Shh, there is no time," Awa pleaded. "Always, remember maam bu góor, great griot Gorgui and how beautiful Lebu'ta is. You must—"

Mambéty stepped between his daughter and nephew. Awa gulped down her thoughts. Adama's eyes were as wide as the sun that raced towards the horizon. Dimly, he felt the weight of Cousin Moustapha's hand on his shoulder. The prince, dazed, moved mechanically with the group. His head pounded and felt as if it would burst.

The cool Atlantic Ocean licked at his feet, and he jumped. He looked around frantically for Awa and saw Uncle Mambéty leading her away. He stopped dead in his tracks. Moustapha's grip tightened on his shoulder.

"Awa!" Adama shouted, his voice was drowned by the screeching caw of the seagulls overhead. Again and again, he screamed her name.

She turned and mouthed something. He could not see her face clearly.

Remember me. Is that what she said? He bellowed incoherently. The salty seawater splashed Adama's face but did not cool his hot tears. Tremors began in his gut and spread. Sea foam swirled around his ankles like leg irons.

"I will find you Adama," Awa's voice was faint, but he heard her clearly. This time he had no doubt. He stood staring. Outstretched arms trembled so violently he resembled an ostrich attempting flight.

Adama's feet quickly rose above the seawater. Cousin Moustapha held him close and spoke in his ear. Hot breath blew melodic sounds that comforted and soothed.

"Mambéty has arranged for you to travel with Jean-Claude to France. Behave yourself and learn much. Endear yourself to le capitaine and gain his trust."

The prince, perched on Moustapha's large arm, stared blankly.

"Come back and avenge your pape and then you will be a worthy

Lamane. My silence of this affair has purchased your life. Become your pape and he may yet live again in you."

Adama's brief solace was interrupted by hands that enveloped his waist. His small body was plucked from Moustapha's embrace.

"Always remember who you are, Adama. Never forget—*you are Lebu'ta!*"

Chapter 40

Hadada Ibis

"Ha, ha, de, dah!" The sound knifed through Adama's consciousness and repeated. "Ha, ha, de, dah!"

The prince lifted his chin from his chest and looked up. Overhead a large, elegant bird flew effortlessly. One of its marbled eyes seemed to be staring at him. He wiped his eyes with the back of his hand and blinked.

The bird opened its large, hooked, black bill and cried again, "Ha, ha, haa dee dah." The Hadada Ibis, covered with rich dark brown plumage, kept pace with the longboat. The white stripe on its head looked like an undulating smile.

To Adama, its call sounded like Djibril's laughter. He searched around the bottom of the boat where colorful rocks and pebbles rolled lazily about. The prince snatched a smooth stone that was nearest to him. He stretched his arm back and hurled it with a grunt. The stone sailed up, curved and nicked the bird's thin leg.

"You are a coward," Bamba said. The Banju laughed, and the bird seemed to agree.

"Ha, haa, de, dah!" The Hadada Ibis broke pace with the boat. It flew quickly towards a small island in the same direction.

Adama watched it fly away with some satisfaction. His eyes followed the bird and inadvertently landed on the island that lay ahead. Even from the boat, Adama could see the fort. The enormous round structure engulfed the north of the small island.

Fort d'Estrées dominated the Vumbi-controlled port. The entire island, barely 89 acres long, housed another fort in the south, known as Le Castel. The two fortifications, replete with many soldiers and cannons, were defenses against other Vumbi and Alkebulon nations on the mainland.

Strong waves rushed at the volcanic rock underneath the large fort. The sea's foamy crest collapsed and receded. The rhythm was steady and loud.

"Ha, ha, de, dah!"

Adama looked skyward. The Hadada Ibis had returned and flew directly above the boat. With its head cocked, the bird's eye seemed to peer down at Adama.

"Ha, ha, de, dah!"

The prince ran his small finger over the ridged contour of Princess Awa's cowrie shell bracelet and squeezed his eyes shut. When he opened them, they fell upon Bamba the Banju who bared his sharp teeth in a menacing grin.

Adama shivered.

Chapter 41

The Horrors of Île de Gorée-Bir

Le capitaine's long, dark auburn hair glistened with grease and sweat. Wild strands broke free of the thin leather tie and tickled Adama's nose. The child inhaled the pungent odor deeply and turned his head searching for fresh air. He found none.

Resting his chin on le capitaine's shoulder, Adama held his breath for what seemed like an eternity. When he could hold it no longer, he gulped down rancid air. He squeezed his eyes shut. The breath taken was worse than his yaye's cleansing tonic of bitter herbs. *Yaye. Had the Waalo really killed her like Bamba said? No.* His mind rejected the possibility.

Adama's tear-filled eyes fell on the oarsmen who hastily pulled up mooring ropes. He, le capitaine, Bamba and the captives had disembarked on the shore just south of Fort d'Estrées' on the northeast flank of the island. As the longboats headed back home, Adama waved gloomily at the oarsmen. No one saw his pitiful gesture. None looked back.

Home. Adama wanted desperately to get home. He ached to see maam bu góor and Awa. *How could they find him so far from*

Lebu'ta? They would need a longboat. What had he done? Why was he being punished? Darkness closed in on him as le capitaine carried him into the walled confines of the fort. Adama held on tightly and wept.

The soldiers on guard at the gate greeted le capitaine Jean-Claude de Visé with grunts. They stared quizzically at the well-dressed Lebu'tan child the seaman carried in his arms.

"Ah, what knavery is this?" snorted a short, stout guard. "Is the boy sick, or has our worthy Capitaine been bewitched by yet another Signare?"

The soldiers snickered.

Adama, intrigued by the Meridional Vumbi dialect, lifted his head to see who was speaking. He blinked eyes red from weeping and beheld a smirking, gray-uniformed guard. The fat Vumbi with the long mustache had a scarred cheek.

"No Métis this!" belched the gray-uniformed guard. "The child is much too dark. Do not worry, Capitaine de Visé. Your secret is safe with me. I will not breathe a word of this to Signare Maguette," he said and led the others in a chorus of laughter.

Jean-Claude put Adama down abruptly. Le capitaine stomped past the soldiers with the prince in tow.

Adama gripped le capitaine's hand. As they penetrated deeper into the fort, the air stagnated. The prince's head swirled. The putrid air was a mixture of rotting flesh, blood, excrement and unwashed bodies. The stench of le capitaine faded from his memory. Bile rose in Adama's throat, and he swallowed hard.

"Where are we?" Adama croaked, but a strong sea breeze swept away his words. The prince swiped tears from his eyes and asked again in a louder voice, "Where are we?" He looked up into le capitaine's lined face expectantly.

Unblinking, Jean-Claude stared down the long, crooked road that lay ahead. As if in a trance, his bloodshot eyes did not waver from the salmon-colored house perched about 200 meters on the left. Adama followed the Frenchman's eyes past the gray cement and brown clay structures to the enchanting single-story house. It shone like a splendid kunzite gemstone nestled between igneous rocks.

Nearer at hand were a riot of guards, prisoners, seamen and merchants. Shouts, screams, wails and laughter collided. The intricately woven colored clothes adorning the Alkebulans clashed with the patternless, heavy clothing of the Vumbi with whom they haggled.

The scarcely clad adult captives struggled and resisted physically and verbally. The guards swore, bludgeoned and pushed. Most of the children huddled together crying and urinating on themselves. Adama stared open-mouthed. His eyes rolled over the faces of the children. *Samba? Malick?* No. His heart sank.

Above the bedlam, Adama heard a slight ringing. He inclined his head. The sound grew more distinct as he and Jean-Claude moved down the road.

"Clang, clang," the rhythmic pounding of hammers on metal was melodic. It grew louder than the tumult and the crashing waves of the great Atlantic. The hypnotic sounds rose and fell cyclically.

The temperature spiked. *Had they walked into an oven?* Perspiration soaked through le capitaine's clothing and bathed his reddened face. Little beads of sweat formed on Adama's forehead as the metalsmith's hut came into view.

From his vantage point, the prince could barely see what the large, dirty man and few boys were doing in the hut. He did see a meaty arm holding a thick, solid hammer high above a balding Vumbi head. It swung down hard and deliberately. Metal clanged loudly, and to Adama it sounded almost like a human cry.

Adama put his free hand over his right ear. The banging reverberated in his small chest. Adama wanted to break free and run down the road. *Run to that pretty house le capitaine eyed.*

Waves of heat from the fire used to soften the metal jabbed at Jean-Claude and Adama like a cattle prod. Steam from the cooling of heated metal in water floated on puffs of smoke. Jean-Claude hurried past the hut. Adama barely had time to notice the shackles, collars, chains and other forged metal devices that hung from the eave.

"What is this place, Monsieur le Capitaine?" Adama pulled his guardian's arm down by the hand he held tightly.

Jean-Claude regarded his charge through hooded green eyes. He smiled briefly.

"Ah, you always have so many questions, mon jeune ami."

Adama was not sure if le capitaine was rebuking him or commending him. He remained quiet.

The pebbles and shells that paved the road slipped between the leather of Adama's sandals and lodged between his toes. He stumbled and limped slightly. Le capitaine did not alter his stride or tempo. The prince quickened his pace. Every other step, Adama shook a foot to rid himself of painful particles of pavement. He dared not fall behind.

The child's head swiveled from side to side. The town, built solely for commerce in flesh, bustled. Smells of urine, feces, and human decay leapt from open doorways and windows. Bound men, women, and children, encouraged by brutal blows, trudged this way and that. Voices uttering protests and pleas in a myriad of languages plucked Adama's ears. He tried to separate and translate words from groans with scant success.

"This is *Île de Gorée*," Le capitaine's voice pierced through the prince's mental calisthenics.

"I do not know the word Gorée."

"No, you would not know that word. This island was once called Goede Reede."

"Goede Reede," Adama repeated, hoping to impress le capitaine with precise pronunciation.

"That is right. You are very good with language, Adama." With his free hand, le capitaine flung sweat from his brow. "Goede Reede is Dutch for good harbor. The Dutch controlled this island once. That was a long time ago, during the time of my Opa Pieter," Jean-

Claude said. "He was a Dutchman and et capitaine." Almost wistfully he declared, "I am very much like my Opa, I think."

The Frenchman and the Lebu'tan child strode briskly past a huddle of chained people taken from the mainland. Small pebbles shifted under their feet. Adama stumbled a bit, then righted himself using le capitaine's steady hand for leverage.

"What is this place?" the child repeated his original question in fluid French.

"It is many things. A port, a warehouse, a trading post."

"Trading post?"

"Yes, it is a place where we barter and trade with the Waalo and others," le capitaine answered offhandedly.

Adama knew something about bartering. Often, he had swapped playthings and knickknacks with Awa and the other children. He also remembered Uncle Mambéty was Waalo. *Uncle Mambéty who Bamba says killed my pape. Had Uncle Mambéty traded him to Monsieur le Capitaine—sold him?*

"Think of it as a marketplace. You have been to market, have you not?"

Adama focused on what le capitaine had asked and nodded in response. Maam bu góor had taken him and Awa to markets where exchanges were made between fishermen, farmers, herders and craftsmen, who were sometimes women. *It was quite exciting. So many people and different smells. Good smells.*

"It is like that," le capitaine said.

Adama looked about for similarity. He saw no fishermen or farmers, no food or goods. Confused, he asked, "What is traded?"

"Oh, that depends. You see those ships?" Jean-Claude gestured towards the sea. "Each one has et capitaine, like me. They come here for slaves. They bring different things to trade to get the slaves."

"Like what?"

"Oh, that depends on who is paying for the voyage. But often it is guns, copper, rum, things like that. Things not already here. Things they cannot get at market."

"Which ship is yours?"

"That one there. Le Bon Dieu. Do you see it?"

Adama peered at vessels anchored off the western shoreline. On the nearest two, privateer slavers had written the ships' names, Good Ship Jesus and Hope in the Lord, on the starboard side. The prince's eyes skipped past these until he beheld Le Bon Dieu.

"Yes," he paused then blurted, "Monsieur le Capitaine I wish to go back home."

"No. No mon jeune ami. I am your guardian now. Your uncle wants me to take you on as an apprentice. There is much I will teach you. Fortunately, it just so happens I am in need of a cabin boy."

Adama's mind raced and tripped over a long-forgotten lesson he had learned. He pouted and said, "You lie to me. This is not Île de Gorée or Goede Reede as you say. This is Bir, or you would say, belly," he continued angrily. "Bir, a Lebu word describing the shape of the island. Maam bu góor said the Lebu are our relatives who lived here before. You see, I do not need you to teach me. My maam bu góor has taught—"

"Your grandfather is not here! If you do not wish to be my apprentice, I will sell you as a slave," le capitaine curled his lip. "You'd do well to learn quickly, for I have many debts!"

Shrieks filled the air punctuating le capitaine's warning. Adama jumped and tightened his grip on Jean-Claude's hand. His breath quickened. The large structures that lined both sides of the road pressed down on the child like a vise. Air filled his lungs hard and fast.

"It is alright, mon jeune ami," said le capitaine more gently. He patted Adam's head gently. "You will get used to it. Come."

The two stepped inside a gray cave-like structure. The hysterical cries became louder. Pleas for help were uttered in many languages and dialects. Adama plucked out many words of distress and shuddered.

The long hall had two entryways on the left, two on the right and one straight ahead. Wooden signs hung above each opening.

Adama read the French words aloud, "Men, women, young girls... What is this place Monsieur le Capitaine? The smell is so bad it chokes the air."

"Detention quarters. Where captives are held," he responded indifferently.

"Oh! How horrible," Adama cried. His mind turned to the longboats and all the people on them. What of Monsieur le Capitaine's threat? *Would he have to live in such a place as this?*

"Boom! Boom!" Le Castel's distant cannon shot, followed by Fort d'Estrées' close report, jolted Adama. The nearby cannon growled like a hippopotamus.

Adama was terrified. "What is that?" Adama asked before bursting into fitful sobs.

Jean-Claude stopped and considered the child. "Come, come," he said. "You are too big for this, mon jeune ami." Crouching down, le capitaine flicked his thumb over the large tears streaming from the prince's eyes. "It is just Le Castel and Fort d'Estrées signaling that all is well."

"Monsieur le Capitaine, I am frightened. Please, may I go home?"

The man scooped Adama up in his arms and turned towards the exit.

"Hush now. I will bring you to Signare Maguette. She will take care of you whilst I make ready for a quick departure." He put the child down.

"Come. You will like Maguette. She is a Métis, very beautiful... almost as beautiful as your yaye. Maguette is also rich from the trade. Besides, I am sure she has some chocolate, and you love chocolate!" Jean-Claude playfully swiped Adama's nose.

Chapter 42

Métis Maguette

The one-story house was the jewel of Fort d'Estrées. It was not the biggest house nor was it the most expensive, but its fuchsia tinted cement was perfectly formed. The windows, adorned with silk imported from China, were just the right size and angle for cool breezes and privacy. It was *the* house and like a shapely woman, it was both admired and envied.

Outside, Adama stood with Jean-Claude. He wondered why le capitaine delayed going inside. The house was quite different from those Adama knew in Lebu'ta. He stared up at the large, ornately carved wooden door. Coated with a black resin, its high gloss shone like the great Atlantic at dusk.

The door opened. The perfume of freshly cut flowers wafted out. Adama's eyes were filled with the vision that was Signare Maguette. She spoke, "Why do you stand in my doorway, Jean-Claude?" The woman's smooth voice was playful. Before le capitaine could answer, she added, "And who do we have here?" She crouched slightly and peered at the child who smiled.

Her scent filled the prince's flared nostrils. The pleasant smell overshadowed the rancid odors he had encountered en route.

Adama gazed into a face like none he had ever seen before. Purplish irises danced in a crystal-clear sea of white. Her eyes beckoned, welcomed and promised refuge. He felt at ease for the first time since leaving Lebu'ta with Malick, Samba and Awa.

"I am Prince Adama N'Diaye of Lebu'ta," Adama said in French. "What is your name?" His eyes were wide.

"How well you speak! My name is Signare Maguette," she said smiling. Her hair was the color of the confection Adama loved so much. She wore a brightly colored yellow, red and green head-wrap. Hair snaked out the back of the scarf tied at the nape of her long neck.

Adama murmured a low guttural sound of awe. The Signare's dark chocolate hair, woven together in large plaits, was striking against her skin. Maguette, a Waalo-French woman, was as shapely as her house.

"You are very beautiful," Adama sighed. He turned to Jean-Claude, "Is she not beautiful Monsieur le Capitaine?" he gushed.

"Well, Capitaine?" Maguette said mischievously. She struck a pose. Her cowrie shell earrings dangled vivaciously.

Jean-Claude's face was red. "Yes, Adama. Maguette is the most beautiful woman in Fort d'Estrées."

The woman's violet eyes darkened to the color of burning coals. "Ha! In Fort d'Estrées? So, who is more beautiful in France, my love? Hmm? Who?" She pushed the words out like a slap.

Adama took a step back. Nervously, he looked at his guardian, Jean-Claude, who took a bold, self-assured step forward, and over the threshold.

The Signare's pronounced Waalo features hardened into a beautiful angry mask. Her eyes challenged Jean-Claude who stood just inches away smiling confidently.

Le capitaine looked back at the prince, "Wait here a moment Adama. Behave yourself. Do not speak to anyone, I will not be a moment."

"No, Adama. Jean-Claude will not be but a moment!" Maguette hissed and slammed the door.

The child listened briefly to the retreating loud voices of le capitaine and la signare. He shrugged, then sat cross-legged with his back against the fuchsia façade. Pleasant flowery smells drifted out the window and settled around him. A cool breeze found its way over the fort's walls and nuzzled his neck.

Adama fell asleep.

Chapter 43

Wait a Moment

"P sst! Psst!"

Adama's eyes fluttered open.

"Son of my sister, help me." The whispered plea was uttered by a man who resembled Bamba the Banju. The short lean man's arms were pulled behind his back and bound at the wrists. He moved swiftly towards the prince. His bare, cracked feet did not stumble on the pebbles and stones he trod upon.

"Bamba?" Adama inquired groggily. *No, it was not Good Bamba.* The face was too round, and his eyes, though the same color, were too wide set.

"Allah save me from idiots and infidels!" The man turned his face heavenward then towards the prince again.

"Are you Banju?" asked Adama in Arabic.

"No time for foolish questions boy. Help me before they come back!" His hazel eyes flared.

Adama remembered how he would not cut Bamba the Banju's binds. He felt afresh Awa's disappointment at his fear. *Not this time.*

Adama hustled to his feet. He reached inside his clothing for his hidden knife. Deep voices, angry and loud, wedged between Adama and the captive.

"Halt!" Two uniformed figures moved quickly towards the prince and the Banju.

"Astaghfirullah! Protect me Allah! Too late," the Banju cried. "They return to kill me!" He ran awkwardly down the road screaming.

The pair of uniformed Vumbi rushed towards them. They looked like the men Adama encountered when le capitaine had carried him into Fort d'Estrées. *The short, fat, gray-uniformed one for certain.* Adama recognized the mustache and worm-like scar on the man's ruddy cheek. The prince shuddered.

Both Vumbi gave Adama a sidelong glance as they gave chase to the Banju who fled down the road. The Vumbi continued to shout words Adama was sure the fleeing Banju did not understand.

Suddenly, the taller man, clad in a blue uniform, doubled back and grabbed Adama. The long-legged Vumbi held the prince under his arm like a parcel.

Adama screamed, "Help!" first in Lebu'tan then quickly switched to French. "M'aider! M'aider, Monsieur le Capitaine de Visé! M'aider!" The words vaporized behind the prince as the Vumbi soldier quickly spirited him away from Signare Maguette's beautiful pink house.

Chapter 44

Spirited Away

Adama was held tightly under his abductor's lean arm. Speedy strides transported him deep into Gorée Island. He felt like an urgent message in the hands of a determined courier. The blue-uniformed Vumbi raced up alleyways and sprinted across roads. Adama's body jerked each time his captor changed direction. The motion was agony and his ribs were rubbed sore.

The guard's coarse blue uniform grated against Adama's small face and obscured much of his vision. Unable to spy any landmarks on the maze of unknown roads, Adama relented and squeezed his eyes shut. He called upon his father's spirit to help him. Immediately his abductor stopped running as if in response to his supplication.

Adama opened his eyes. Part of a ramshackle door filled his vision. Keys jangled and metal scraped metal. The guard muscled the door open and threw him into darkness. The door slammed shut, and the lock clicked.

Adama lay on his back and felt the coolness of the packed dry earth. Sunlight shone through the spaces and cracks in the lone door. There was no other opening.

The earthen floor seemed to open wide and swallow him whole. His breath quickened. Fear became his master. He felt as if he had been buried alive.

"Pape, help me!" His strangled cry plucked the stagnant air. To Adama, his pape, the great prince Cheikh Anta N'Diaye, personified strength and courage.

"Pape, Yaye," he croaked. Adama tried to conjure an image of the faces he remembered. His yaye's smooth, dark skin. His pape's low hairline and clear eyes. Their smiling faces flickered briefly in Adama's mind.

"Calm yourself Adama," the disembodied voice filled the room.

Startled, Adama's breath caught in his throat. On a beam of sunlight that slipped through the door, he could see his parents.

"You must use the strength of our ancestors' spirits," said the low deep voice.

Adama's fingers stroked the air. His parents' features collided, melted and transformed into the image of maam bu góor. He realized that it was the Lamane's voice he heard.

"I am frightened, maam bu góor," Adama said. "There is so little light, and I am alone. I am lost!"

"Light the flame within you and see that you are never alone. The ancestors surround you and offer their strength. Use the strength of our ancestors' spirits," the voice trailed off.

The beam of sunlight expanded and dissolved his grandfather's face. "Do not go maam bu góor," Adama said. "No!" The light receded out of the room.

Adama sprang up and charged the door. It seemed to push him back, and he landed hard on the dirt floor. Adama rammed the door again with no success. He pressed his face against it and peered through the crack. No one was about. No noise was heard.

"I am in here! I am in here! Save me," Adama screamed repeatedly as loudly as he could in French. He put his ear to the door. There was no reply. Dejectedly, he threw himself down and wept.

In the dark, Adama's thoughts recalled the Banju outside La

Signare Maguette's house. The man had said the guards wanted to kill him. *I tried to be brave and save the Banju. Who will save me?*

"Awa," he whimpered. Tears fell on the cowrie shell bracelet the princess had fastened to his wrist.

"Boom!" Nearby, a cannon was discharged. Adama jumped. The report was deafening and followed by another blast.

Adama covered his ears and scooted backward. "Ancestors, help me! I am lost," the prince cried. The back of his head hit a wall.

The artillery stopped, and the room became quiet again. Monsieur le Capitaine had told him the cannons were fired several times each sunrise. It was a signal of some kind. Adama could not remember what. He set his mind to remember but drifted off into a dream until the gruff voices of his captors shook him awake.

Chapter 45

Garrison Guards

The room was small. A couple of straw pallets flanked a dirty wash basin and potty. A large hurricane lantern sat atop a makeshift table. It cast long shadows about the room and a shifting dark menace over two pale-faced men.

The garrison guards spoke in hushed tones. The men sat on rickety, rough wooden stools at a bedraggled table. Each clutched a tankard filled with watered-down ale like an unwilling bride. The lanky, blue-uniformed man mopped his face with bony hands. The knotted joints on his splayed fingers resembled an orb spider's web.

The paunchy, gray-uniformed man took a pull of the vile liquid and sucked the excess from his mustached lips before speaking. "Jean-Claude de Visé will certainly come looking for le petit garçon," the fat guard said. "Oui! Did you not see how le capitaine carried him in his arms with such care?"

"Ah! Let Jean-Claude look," replied the blue-uniformed guard. "I heard his crew say they make a hasty departure. He will not spare too much time searching for le petit garçon."

"You are so sure of yourself. Always with you, it's something.

What made you do it? Trouble. Désastre! Always," the worm-like scar on his cheek squirmed as he spat on the dirt floor, "trouble!"

"No, no, no mon ami. We have no worries. Besides, you are the one who is always so hungry. Oui. Complain about lack of food all the time. Do you know how much meat and ale he is worth!"

The fat guard's belly rumbled in agreement. "Le bon. But we cannot keep him here. No, no, no. Where to hide him?"

The blue-uniformed guard grinned. "With Signare Alimatou, of course." He twisted his scrawny, turkey-like neck and winked at the prince in the corner. The guard's yellow eyes and teeth seemed to glow.

Adama shivered. He was sure that these Vumbi men were cannibals. The hungry way they looked at him was carnivorous. The fat one's belly kept growling. *Will they cook me after they kill me or will they eat me raw?*

The rotund guard frowned. "And if we are caught?" The question went unanswered. Neither man wanting to think about the possibilities. Punishment for soldiers and seaman alike was brutal, torturous, and sometimes deadly. It was too late to back out, but he could always turn the situation to his advantage. His friend was, after all, un imbécile.

"Whatever you do," the fat guard said, "until Jean-Claude leaves Fort d'Estrées and is far out to sea, no harm to him" his voice rose. "Oui! I say not a hair on le petit garçon's head shall be lost. No, no, no, mon ami. Or you may lose yours!"

Adama shook with fear. He understood enough of the Meridional Vumbi dialect to know the danger at hand. He felt for the knife in his clothing. It was there, but, like him, it was too small to make a difference.

The prince sighed. *Will le capitaine find me? These are wicked violent men. Cannibals for certain. It is just as griot Gorgui said.* Silently, Adama called upon his pape's spirit again to help him.

"That Alimatou, ah ha! But she is une femme difficile, no?" asked the fat guard.

"Hmm. Oui! But she is just what we need. She is une femme without the scruples, mon ami," replied the blue-uniformed guard. "Ah, ha, ha! What she lacks in scruples she has in money!"

"I agree. But do you know how la femme got her money?"

The thin guard shook his large head.

"Ah. It was her husband who gave her the start. She was from the lower classes. Practically a slave in her own land. But la femme was very beautiful. Oui, the most beautiful femme—"

"Ahh," the thin guard said waiving his hand dismissively. "Mon ami, you take too long to tell a story."

"Ha, ha. You are correct. Signare Alimatou married a merchant from Nantes. He was a factor and did a pretty good business up until he died a few years ago."

"What did he die of? She give him something?"

"No, no. You have the head of an ant! Are you going to listen or are you going to ask stupid questions?" Snapped the fat guard. "It was the malaria. That is what people die from here. But, Monsieur le docteur always says the death is from malaria. So, who knows?" He shrugged his meaty shoulders.

"Ahh," the thin guard said. "Go on, go on."

"Oui. But before he died, Signare Alimatou convinced him to buy the land behind the house. He did not think much of the land as part of it had lots of rocks and boulders. But he bought it anyway. For her, he would do anything.

"When he died, Signare Alimatou sectioned the land. She took the men she held for slavers and uses them to quarry the rocks. She sells the rocks to le commandant du Fort d'Estrées. Le commandant uses the rocks and boulders to expand the fort. All the while she is collecting from the sellers and the buyers for brokering the trade and for holding the slaves. Smart? Eh?"

"Ahh, I see," the thin guard nodded.

"Ah, ha. She uses another section to grow food to feed the slaves she is holding. Les femmes and les enfants are set to farming. This keeps the slaves from idleness, and she charges for feeding them too.

Magnifique! La femme, she is no fool, I tell you. Tread carefully with that one, mon ami."

"Ahh! In the end she is just la femme. Signare or no. Just another femme. And a Waalo too. Not even a Métis like Maguette."

"She hates Maguette."

"I do not know why. She has more money than Maguette."

"Women are strange that way. Always in competition over foolish petty things. But that is not our affair. We can use it to our advantage. She knows about Maguette and Jean-Claude and hates one for the love of the other. Come—let us go. Get le petit garçon," commanded the fat guard.

The thin guard slid back from the makeshift table. His stool drew uneven lines in the dirt floor. He grabbed a bag that hung from a nail and approached the prince.

Adama pressed his back hard against the wall. He screamed with all his might as the guard advanced towards him.

Everything went dark. A rucksack tossed over Adama's head cut off the lantern's light as well as much of the air. The sensation of rapid movement disconcerted him for a moment. Then he felt the bag pressed against his nostrils. Adama struggled to breathe. The rucksack was as hot as the metalsmith's hut. Stifling, the prince's small fingers clawed at the woven cloth. His frantic scratches yielded no results.

The sensation of being carried slowed then stopped. Adama felt his body being thrown. His head hit something hard and began to swell. The growing lump throbbed. Moist hot air greeted his feet. His lower extremities poked out of the bag. Upper extremities and head were still confined. He wriggled and twisted. The rucksack was roughly yanked off his body and over his head.

Air! Greedily, the prince sucked in breath after breath. His mind whirled then focused on the voices.

Three voices. An enchanting new face.

Adama listened quietly to the two guards ask a woman if they might have an audience with Signare Alimatou. The woman, who must have been a servant, departed.

He inhaled deeply and mentally absorbed his new surroundings. The beautiful room, filled with a floral scent, was more than twice as big as the guard's shack.

Momentarily, a tall lean woman sauntered into the room. Her hands busily straightened her headdress as if she had just tied it on. It was made of expensive-looking green cotton threaded with gold. The headdress covered the many small plaits, adorned with beads and cowrie shells, that cascaded down her back.

The woman's bearing was regal and seemed to be expectant of obedience. Her soft features were sharpened by the deep angle of her eyes. Her mannerisms were precise. She looked lovely in her matching buba and kaftan wrapper. Adama knew this must be Signare Alimatou. He recalled Signare Maguette's home and wondered if all the women of Bir were pretty and smelled like flowers.

Chapter 46

Signare Alimatou

"**B**onjour," Signare Alimatou greeted the uniformed guards warily. She turned her gaze to the young, dirty prince who had been dumped in her quarters. "What is going on? Who is this le petit garçon and why do you bring him here?" she asked curtly.

The lanky guard spoke too quickly, making it difficult for Signare Alimatou to interpret his French. The fat one, twirling his mustache, said nothing.

Signare Alimatou understood the gist of the request. The guards wanted her to house the child until le capitaine Jean-Claude de Visé departed Gorée Island. *But why?*

"Speak more slowly," she commanded. "Your dialect is too rough for my ears. Tell me, what is le petit garçon to Jean-Claude?"

"That is difficult to explain. Le petit garçon arrived here this morning with le capitaine," said the sizable fat guard, speaking for the first time.

"If he is with Jean-Claude then how did you two come to possess him? Fort d'Estrées' guards are to protect the trade, not engage in it!" she snapped.

"Of course, you are correct. Oui, Oui. Most certainly. I, er, we found him outside of Signare Maguette's house," said the thin guard.

"Found him? You do not find people on Gorée Island," Signare Alimatou retorted.

"What he means to say is—"

The Signare cut him off. "You stole him from Jean-Claude." She punctuated her surmise with a dark stare.

The fat guard looked nervous. The scar on his cheek seemed to squirm under the Signare's fixed gaze.

She smiled. "You stole him and now you wish to hide him here. Ha, ha! Jean-Claude will probably have to borrow more money from Maguette to compensate for this loss. She will not like that. She will never get it back." Her raven-black eyes danced above a gleaming white smile. "It is like paying a lover for love. C'est magnifique. Ha, ha. Marvelous!"

The thin guard and the fat guard exchanged grins.

"Une petit garçon is worth much," said Alimatou sharply. "What is my profit?"

"A third," the blue-uniformed guard said louder than the fat guard's offer of a fourth.

"Ha, ha, ha!" Alimatou laughed. "One half! And be careful not to insult me again. I am no novice here. I built this," she gestured expansively with both hands, "not my husband."

"We meant no insult, Signare. No, no," said the fat guard, who bowed deeply. He elbowed the thin guard, who followed suit.

"Just so we understand each other. Take le petit garçon out back and give him to one of de femmes. What is his name?"

"My name is Prince Adama N'Diaye," Adama said in very perfect French.

Signare Alimatou's head jerked around.

"I am the grandson of Kilifa Ibrahima N'Diaye, Great Lamane of Lebu'ta. Good Signare Alimatou, please help me return home."

Three mouths dropped open in quick succession.

Signare Alimatou composed herself quickly and hissed, "What trouble is this you bring to my house!"

The Vumbi men stammered incoherently.

"Le petit garçon! He never said a word before," said the fat guard.

"I did not know he spoke French," added the thin guard.

"Get him out back quickly you fools!"

Signare Alimatou's mind ignited. The child was a prince. Possibly a future Lamane.

Much royalty passed through her gates, but from defeated kingdoms not from the strength that was Lebu'ta. Worse, it was said that the Lamane did not condone the trade and supported Nasir Al-Din's jihad against it.

Would Lamane Kilifa N'Diaye unite with Al-Din and launch an attack against Fort d'Estrées in search of le petit garçon? I could be killed, for pity's sake.

I will seek out the Lamane. Yes. He would be grateful and indebted to me. But maybe he would not see things quite that way. Perhaps I should get him back to Jean-Claude. Ah! Blasted politics. Idiot guards. I must decide quickly.

Too bad I cannot keep the boy. His talent for language is much needed in my business. Besides, I have no children and could have trained and groomed him as my own. Blessings are always so few.

"Oh," sighed Signare Alimatou. "No peace for the peaceful. No benefit for the beneficent!"

Chapter 47

Selling Chiefs and Warriors

S idy, Al-Din's Baol war chief, smashed a huge rock against a boulder. He imagined it was the fat head of that dart-blowing raider, Garmi. Bits of rock splinters cut Sidy's unflinching face. *Garmi you snake!*

He searched for another large rock and brought it down hard. Too hard. Sidy felt as if he had pulled a muscle in his back. He arched it and felt the flat metal collar cut into his neck. The device was bolted shut less than two sunrises ago when Garmi sold him, and hundreds of his best men, on Gorée Island.

Sidy ran meaty fingers under the collar. He sneered at the blood on his fingertips. The collar and two meters long iron chains were a soldier's humiliation. Each chain ended at the side of a collar and began anew on the opposite side. Sidy looked out at the sea of collared Baol soldiers, strung together by chains, busting rocks for the Vumbi cannibals.

After a successful battle and decisive win against the King of Waalo, he and his fellow warriors celebrated their victory. Perhaps they celebrated too long and too hardily, but it was a bloody fight with many casualties.

The war chief had to concede that the Waalo tactic showed great cunning. Garmi's underhanded moonlight raid caught him and his men completely off guard. *A fine reward for leniency and decency on the battlefield!*

Many good soldiers and fine horses were senselessly slaughtered. The Waalo were known to be jealous of Baol's superior horsemen. The raid would not overturn Baol's triumph over Waalo, but it would weaken the Baol Kingdom considerably and proved a great embarrassment for Sidy.

Garmi had no respect for the rules of combat. Now here they were in this pit, reduced to busting rocks and rolling water barrels. An honorable soldier's death was his right. *Ha! Chained and branded. Disgrace. At least Good Zenaga died in battle.*

The war chief tugged the iron chain. *When we escape from this island, we will show Waalo no mercy. Ah! I will crush Garmi's head with my bare hands.*

Sidy smashed another rock and considered strategy. They must move quickly. *If the Vumbi cannibals moved us to one of the ships... well it would just make things more difficult.*

The smell of sticks and wood burning pulled the war chief's attention from revenge to hunger. He glanced at the women captives who were preparing to cook scraps for him and his men to eat. The sound of wooden spoons striking metal pots was inspirational. *The talking drum!*

He looked for another rock and scouted a perfect one. It was heavy but not quite as big as the others. Sidy banged it against the boulder, hard then soft, scrape then sharp. *Would they recognize the code?*

The men nearest to the war chief paused their toil briefly. They listened. Each mimicked the message sending it down the line to be picked up and shared. *Success! I can all but feel Garmi's head in my hands.* He grinned. The war chief's bared teeth were indeed terrible to behold.

Chapter 48

Lost and Found

"Yes, Monsieur. I understand," said Oumou, a plump woman with big sad eyes. She took Adama by the hand.

"You see that," the thin guard pointed over Adama's shoulder.

Adama turned his head. A Vumbi held a girl who was no bigger than himself. She wriggled and fought. Another Vumbi pulled a long iron stick from a furnace. The bent end, glowing red and white, was pushed against the girl's small arm. Adama saw a puff of smoke, heard her scream and watched her legs give way. He gasped and squeezed Oumou's hand tightly.

"Behave yourself or I will have you branded like her," the thin guard pinched Adama's shoulder, "and collared too."

"Ow," Adama cried out and winced.

Oumou moved a bit so her body partially shielded Adama from the thin guard.

"No, no Monsieur. The boy will be no trouble. Come little one, Good Oumou will watch over you." The woman led Adama away from the guard and further into Alimatou's slave holding curtilage.

The thin guard sneered at Adama and went back inside Signare Alimatou's house.

Oumou settled Adama near the fence that separated the quarry from the cooking area. "You must be hungry. I will feed you soon." She caressed his face with rough hands, smiled slightly and returned to her chores.

Adama sat cross-legged on the ground. *What to do? Escape. Yes, I will run away. I have my knife tucked away for protection. Maybe I can find a longboat and get home. But how?*

Although he knew it was nearby, Adama could not see nor smell the ocean. He looked about the vast area behind Signare Alimatou's house for a clue. No steps that might lead down to the water. Lots of fencing arranged in curves and lines.

Adama could see clearly how the fences defined where the men worked, the women cooked, and the vegetables were planted. It was similar to how the fat guard had described the curtilage to the thin guard. Except he had not mentioned the area where Vumbi with iron sticks, burned the flesh of children and even adults. Beyond the Vumbi was the only visible exit. *How can I get through without being burned on the arm?*

The pleasant smell of food cooking pushed the question from his mind. A slow burn ignited in the pit of his stomach. His mouth filled with warm, tart saliva. He would eat first, find a different exit and a way down to the sea. If anyone tried to stop him, he would cut them with his knife. But he was so hungry.

Adama coughed lightly, hoping to get Oumou's attention. He coughed louder, and she soon handed him a rough, wooden-hewn bowl of soup and a piece of bread. The food smelled like his yaye's steamed okra and fonio. He smiled.

He looked at the bread and frowned. Mold had taken hold of the crust. Adama's stomach moved about loudly. He had not eaten in a long while. He scraped off the green growth with his thumbnail and dipped the bread into the soup. The thin liquid undulated and jostled the small pieces of root vegetables. He peered into the bowl. No okra. No fonio.

Adama wanted to dash the bowl to the ground. He felt eyes upon him and turned abruptly. A girl behind a fence stared at him. Her puffy, red, almond-shaped eyes held his gaze, then dropped to the bowl in his hand. Adama frowned, looked down at the soup, then at the girl again. He knew her face. She was the girl whom the Vumbi had poked with the glowing iron stick. Recognition sparked compassion.

Bowl and bread in hand, Adama got to his feet. He advanced towards the girl. She sat apart from the several other children in Signare Alimatou's slave holding pen.

The fence, much taller than either child, stood sentinel between them. Adama sat as close as he could. He dipped some bread in the soup and passed it through the fence. She reached to get it, whimpered, then switched hands.

Adama saw at once that her arm, damaged and swollen, caused her great pain to move. His eyes struggled not to linger on its oozing white blisters.

They sat without speaking. Adama continued to feed the girl and ate a little himself. He looked past her to the other children. He was surprised none of them rushed to share his food. Eerily, none of them seemed to be aware of his presence. Their faces were frightening masks of horror and confusion darkened by despair.

Adama trembled and looked away. He thought about the times he and his friends sat together listening to griot Gorgui. It seemed so long ago. Something tapped in the back of his mind.

Amidst the noises of the women cooking and the men quarrying rocks, Adama heard a pattern.

The pattern danced in his mind like words. There it was again, repeating. It was griot Gorgui's talking drum! No, impossible.

Adama listened. The diversion took him inward to a place in his mind that was familiar and happy. The thumping transformed into vocalizations then translated into language. Adama looked about.

Beyond Oumou and the other women were men busting rocks. They were making the rocks speak like the talking drum. How clever. None of the women or other children seemed to recognize the words. He smiled.

The girl grunted and opened her mouth wide like a hatchling. Adama shoved more bread through the fence. A shadow cast over both him and the girl. They looked up.

"So here you are mon jeune ami," said Jean-Claude.

Startled, Adama scrambled to his feet tipping the bowl over. The girl looked jealously at the ground that quickly devoured the remaining soup.

"Monsieur le Capitaine! You found me at last," Adama said. He embraced Jean-Claude warmly.

Chapter 49

Gain His Trust

"Well, well. Who is this pretty little one you romance with food? What of your dear Awa?" asked Jean-Claude. He looked down at Adama smiling. "You are generous with victuals like your yaye."

Confusion assaulted Adama's thoughts. A twinge of guilt nipped at his still mostly empty stomach. Had he betrayed Awa? No. Awa would have wanted him to share his food.

Adama looked back at the girl. She had not moved from where they had sat separated by the fence. It came to him that he had never heard her speak. He tried to remember if he had seen her tongue.

"May she come with us, Monsieur le Capitaine? I will watch over her," Adama said.

Jean-Claude brayed a deep laugh. The dark lines etched under his green eyes burrowed yet deeper. He picked up Adama and walked towards Signare Alimatou's house.

"You wicked petit garçon," Jean-Claude said. "I am sick with worry and you are sick with love. Ah! But the makings of a Frenchman you already have!"

Adama said nothing. He thought it best not to tell le Capitaine that he did not desire to become a Vumbi. He did not want to appear ungrateful.

Jean-Claude stopped walking. He spoke in a whisper directly into Adama's ear. "Tell me quickly, how did you come to be here? Did I not tell you to wait and speak to no one?" Jean-Claude's question communicated a harsh rebuke.

"Oui, Monsieur le Capitaine. I spoke to no one. Guards attacked a Banju man in front of Good Signare Maguette's house and grabbed me too. They wanted to *sell* me," Adama said aghast.

He searched le capitaine's face for a sign of empathetic outrage at this horrific possibility. Jean-Claude's facial expression did not change. It was then Adama remembered le capitaine had threatened to sell him too. Perhaps he would make good on that threat.

Anxiously, Adama said, "They brought me here to Signare Alimatou's. I told her who I was, but she did not believe me and I was sent out back. That is how I met the pretty girl who does not speak."

"Ah ha!" said Jean-Claude knowingly. The pair stood just outside Signare Alimatou's house. "You told Alimatou your name?"

"Yes," Adama said quietly. He thought it best not to tell Monsieur le Capitaine that he had asked Signare Alimatou to help him get home.

Jean-Claude put Adama down. "Wait here," he instructed.

Adama grabbed Jean-Claude's hand.

"Do not worry, mon jeune ami, no one will steal you from here."

Adama watched Jean-Claude disappear inside the house. He was not comforted by le capitaine's words. *Why were people stolen from their families and friends?* He turned. Slowly his eyes navigated down the slope of the land. The sea of undulant, bent brown bodies in Signare Alimatou's yard seemed to call out to him. His attention anchored on the men who continued to communicate by banging the rocks they quarried.

In the excitement of Jean-Claude's appearance, Adama had forgotten the thumps and bumps he had interpreted. The sounds sailed through the air. The tempo and volume had changed. Adama listened and nodded. Baol. Certainly Baol.

Adama remembered the Baol warrior-scouts who had freed some of the captives. *That was right before Bamba the Banju took Awa and me,* he thought. *And griot Gorgui taught us that the Baol Kingdom had been part of the Jolof Empire many dry seasons past. Both Baol and Lebu'ta share Wolof and Serer heritages.*

"Oh," Adama said aloud, "Both languages are similar."

Adama had no trouble understanding what the Baols were communicating with their makeshift talking drums. The Baol would escape tonight and bring death to Signare Alimatou and all Vumbi. They would take over the fort.

These mighty soldiers from the southwest would surely kill Monsieur le Capitaine. Would they kill the girl too? Worse, would they kill me? What to do? He remembered the Baol's deadly talon blade and thought, *I dare not take the risk.*

Adama remembered Good Cousin Moustapha said he must please Monsieur le Capitaine and gain his trust. Perhaps telling about the Baol message he was listening to was the way to do both.

Yes. He would warn le capitaine. *Surely le capitaine would be grateful and put me on a longboat for home. And the girl. Yes, I will ask again for the girl. She could come and live in Lebu'ta with me.*

Adama felt the weight of the cowrie shell bracelet. He thought of Awa, then his mind drifted to delicious food from home—okra and fonio. Voices from inside the signare's house interrupted Adama's musings.

He walked closer to the pen where he could see the girl who did not speak. He smiled and waved. She did not return the salute. Adama frowned and debated whether he should shout. It seemed as though she was looking at him. Perhaps not.

"Still flirting with that pretty little one. Eh?" Jean-Claude questioned Adama from the doorway.

Adama's face became hot.

"Come, it is time for us to go. We must make haste. While you were here courting, my men made ready Le Bon Dieu."

"I was not courting. I was only being friendly," said Adama. He cast furtive glances at the girl.

"I know all about how friendly garçons are with filles. Come, come. It is folly to delay with slaves aboard ship."

Adama hustled over to the house.

"Monsieur le Capitaine. Monsieur le Capitaine. I have something to tell you in your ear!"

From behind the fence the little girl's almond-shaped eyes followed Adama's movements intently. She watched every word his mouth formed.

Chapter 50

Rebellion

Sidy was satisfied that his plan was foolproof. At sunset, they would strike. The initial attack would be quick and quiet. Then the real fight would begin. In the end, the entire island would be theirs. He was sure of this.

The guards were slack in their discipline. His men were battle-tested, true and eager to avenge themselves on Waalo. A much worthier opponent than these Vumbi barbarians who burned the flesh of women and children.

What folly to have such long chains between the men. Did they not see it was a weapon? Sidy smiled inwardly. Earlier he had instructed his men surreptitiously by tapping rocks.

The orders were simple. Use the chains as garrotes. Coordinate movements like bukki pack hunters. Wrap the chains around the guards' necks. Pull until the necks crack or the eyes pop. Be swift. Do not let a cry escape their Vumbi lips.

Sidy looked skyward. He observed the sun retreat from the rising night sky. It was almost time. He picked up another rock and felt his muscles contract. Spasms shot through his back. His neck burned, propelling his mind forward to the challenges ahead.

The collars. They must find keys to the metal collars. One of the guards should have a key in a pocket. One key would be enough to get started. Sidy was confident more keys would be found in the guards' shack.

His men would find the keys and he would be rid of this blasted contraption. Sidy touched the lock on the metal collar. Soon he and his men would be in battle again. Combat. Glorious combat, suitable for Baol soldiers. Escape the confines of the quarry. Move to the fort and take control of the munitions store. Swiftly rout the Vumbi. *Ah, then on to Waalo!*

Sidy envisioned Garmi's surprise. This time, Baol's soldiers would overrun Waalo's villages and countryside alike. There would be no mercy. His heart ached for battle like a lovesick boy for a woman's tender touch. He pulled his mind back to the present moment. First the Vumbi. It was time.

The ground shook slightly. The sounds of men marching were unmistakable.

They were exposed. *How?* His mind skipped over the unimportant question. Sidy knew he had to act fast. Victory alone was his focus. He howled the Baol battle signal. His men took up the cry and immediately attacked the guards.

Sidy leapt at the guard nearest to him. Speedily, he wrapped his length of chain around the fat uniformed neck. The iron links jangled as he and the Baol soldier to his left pulled hard. He heard the small bones in the guard's neck crack. Sidy unwound the chain and let the body collapse onto the ground. He knelt down and scouted the fallen man's pocket for a key. Tobacco, bread and a measure of cheese tumbled out. Sidy plunged into the other pocket. A small bag of gunpowder and a few steel balls for the pistol tied to the dead guard's waist. No key.

Several guards ran past. Sidy reached out and took hold of the nearest fleeing leg. The guard tumbled down on his side like a felled antelope. His body covered his unsheathed sword.

The guard rolled onto his face and moved as if to push himself up. A steely glint drew Sidy's eyes to the guard's sword. Sidy threw his weight on top of the guard and crushed him into the earth. The guard bucked and gyrated and yelled out for help. Sidy struck the side of the guard's head fiercely with a chain-covered fist. He straddled the prone body and rained blows on the guard's head until blood flowed freely.

Sidy turned the corpse over and rifled the pockets. His long fingers felt cool metal. A key! Hurriedly, he pulled it out. He motioned to the Baol soldier chained next to him. Sidy struggled to insert the key. Finally the metal collar clicked open. Sidy shoved the key into the Baol soldier's hand. In turn, the soldier unlocked Sidy's collar. Sidy took a brief moment to rub his sore abraded neck. He picked up the sword and immediately reassessed the situation.

Most of his Baol soldiers were rid of the metal collars. Some fought with the swords taken from dead guards. Others continued to use the chains to good effect. Baol seemed to have the advantage.

The ground shook more violently. Sidy knew the fort soldiery was close at hand. Trapped in the quarry, they would be like lions in a hole. It was impossible to get behind the enemy. Probably equally unlikely to manage even a single flank. The only option that came to mind was to split the attack. If he could get at least some men to the munitions store, victory was still possible.

Sidy observed one of the younger men going about confiscating pistols, steel balls and gunpowder. He shouted to him to give the pistols to the maimed and wounded. Tell them to get up on high boulders and be at the ready.

Two cannons, pushed by French soldiers from the fort, rolled into view. Sidy looked around wildly for the formation of his men. Too many remained in the depressed center of the quarry. He took a deep breath from his diaphragm and wailed. The answer from the Baol soldiers was like thunder.

The orders spilled from Sidy's mouth like a geyser. Fourscore Baol soldiers vaulted over the fences. Their feet stampeded past the children and trampled but a few. The silent girl with the almond-shaped eyes was not amongst them.

"Boom, boom!" The volleyed cannonballs smashed into the quarry's rock wall. It began to crumble as the French soldiers took aim and fired their single-shot pistols. A number of Sidy's men were killed or badly wounded.

Sidy observed that the Vumbi soldiers did not attempt to enter the quarry. His worst fear realized. They were like fish in a net. There was but one chance that his men could get through. Should he sacrifice more Baol soldiers or wait for another opportunity?

The decision was made for him. Just before the enemy attacked in earnest, Sidy heard one of his men—who sounded like good Zenaga—give the Baol warriors the signal. The Vumbi soldiers overran Signare Alimatou's property like ants on a warm carcass.

Sidy bellowed for Baol to counterattack. This final command but past his lips when a steel ball shot through his throat. His last thought was of Garmi.

Chapter 51

Middle Passage

The longboat slid across the great Atlantic Ocean. Its oarsmen, anxious to conclude their ninth and final voyage of the day, pushed the foamy water behind them vigorously. The men, brothers by birth and fishermen by trade, often transported captives from the island, they called Bir, to the ships, they called tombs.

It was a dirty business, but unavoidable. True, the duo regularly provided ships' tender, but neither was foolish enough to trust the privateers who engaged them. With good reason. It was widely known that even those who captured and sold mainland people to the Vumbi could find themselves aboard slave ships—never seen again.

According to the griots, danger and death disembarked from the first ships that arrived more than 200 dry seasons ago. From that point till now the lives of the fishermen and families living along the coast were riddled with an ever-present peril. Capture. Disappearance.

In the beginning, the fishermen did not understand the intent of the Vumbi sailors. Now they were known as cannibals who came by sea.

The longboat was nearly upon Le Bon Dieu. Wails and curses became louder the nearer they drew to the ship. The Dutch-built fluyt bobbed on anchor like a floating corpse.

The oarsmen and their three passengers heard the cannon fire. One from nearby Fort d'Estrées, the other from the more distant Le Castel. Both Adama and the girl with the almond-shaped eyes jolted at the booming sounds. The signals between the two Vumbi installations ceased as abruptly as they began. All was well on the Vumbi-controlled island.

For a moment, silence reigned. Even the noise from Le Bon Dieu seemed to stop. It was as if all sound from the island and the continent that lay beyond it paused to give obeisance to another departing prince.

Jean-Claude observed the consternation of the two children. "Do not worry. It is just le commandant signaling he put down the revolt you uncovered. Such a clever boy you are Adama," Jean-Claude patted Adama's head. "Le Commandant paid well for the information. And I have paid you," he said looking at the girl. "But you must give her a name. What shall we call her?"

Adama thought that the girl who did not speak must have a name already. He did not want to rename his new friend. That would be impolite, but he did not want to appear ungrateful.

The light rush of water on oars stopped.

"Aicha," he blurted out just as the longboat tapped the side of Le Bon Dieu. "We shall call her Aicha."

Part Six

Lebu'tan Luminosity

"A people without the knowledge of their past history, origin and culture is like a tree without roots."

—Marcus Garvey

Chapter 52

Dame Returns

United States, North America — 21st Century

Dame's consciousness glided over Le Bon Dieu. Quite clearly he could see Adama, the little girl the prince called Aicha, and Jean-Claude walking on deck. Bamba was there too—below deck in the slave hold. Above deck, crewmen scurried about readying the Dutch-built fluyt for its long voyage.

As the anchor rose and broke through the waves, Dame descended into a sea of great sadness. That sight, coupled with the wails of the captives, overwhelmed him. Dame found himself unable to telepathically turn another page of the sacred book as he had been doing.

Time contracted and catapulted Dame forward. Beneath him, wavy ocean blues receded like a tsunami. Then, with great force, subdivisions, skyscrapers, and freeways crashed into view. Dame found he was screaming as his consciousness plummeted back into his body which sat in his kitchen near parted paisley curtains.

The open book, still in Dame's hands, had no writing on either page. Abruptly, the ancient book slammed shut, and the glow emanating from its copper cover dimmed.

Dame could not see the glyph that hung from his nostril. He shook his head to clear his mind, and it flew off and dissolved in flight. "I must find the children!" he said and got to his feet.

Also by J.C. Moore

Quick Fic, Short Shorts

And Other Great Beginnings

(Compilation)

Don't Fall Asleep

(Novel)

Time to G.I.T: Quick Speaking Guides

(Self-Help)

Oh! Could You Imagine?

(Children's Picture book)

I am crocodile!

(Children's Illustrated Storybook)

Acknowledgments

I thank Pixabay.com for providing access to free images and photos without encumbrance. I appreciate the portal and all who contribute their work without charge.

Special thanks to contributor MasterTux 3d Artist for the map art used as the basis for the front cover. This work has added visual richness to this book.

About the Author

J.C. Moore is an author and literary activist whose work explores social and spiritual issues. She writes ethnic fiction, children's books, screenplays, and nonfiction literary works. Her book *I am Crocodile!* won the 2018 AAGHS International Book Award. Other titles include *Oh! Could You Imagine*, *Don't Fall Asleep*, *Time to GIT Guide*, *Quick Fic: Short Shorts and Other Great Beginnings*, and *The Light-Bearer and the Darkness* series.

jcmoore.com